THE HUNT

BROTHERHOOD PROTECTORS WORLD

DESIREE HOLT

Copyright © 2021, Desiree Holt

Formatting by Wizards in Publishing

Cover by Croco Designs

This book is a work of fiction. Names, characters, places and incidents are products of the author's imagination or used fictitiously. Any resemblance to actual events, locales or persons living or dead is entirely coincidental.

© 2021 Twisted Page Press, LLC ALL RIGHTS RESERVED

No part of this book may be used, stored, reproduced or transmitted without written permission from the publisher except for brief quotations for review purposes as permitted by law.

This book is licensed for your personal enjoyment only. This book may not be re-sold or given away to other people. If you would like to share this book with another person, please purchase an additional copy for each recipient. If you're reading this book and did not purchase it, or it was not purchased for your use only, please purchase your own copy.

To former SEAL Jack Carr, sniper, team leader, who is the epitome of what a SEAL is and should be—honor, integrity, courage, respect. A man I am honored to call friend. He is now a New York Times best selling author using his knowledge and experience to create breath stealing novels.

THANK YOU

Thank youTo those who help me labor, who support me in the toughest hours, who encourage me, who brighten my day and make it all worthwhile: Margie Hager who reads it all in its rawest form; to Steven Horwitz, without a doubt the best most supportive son in the world; to my daughters Suzanne Hurst and Amy Nease for their unflagging encouragement and support. And to Maria Connor, world's best assistant, without whom there would be no Desiree Holt.

To Elle James, for inviting me into her World and sharing her characters with me.

Last but far from least, to you, my wonderful readers, who take this journey with me every day and who have made writing my books a blessing.

Where can you find me:

THANK YOU

www.facebook.com/desireeholtauthor
www.facebook.com/desiree01holt
Twitter @desireeholt
Pinterest: desiree02holt
Google: https://g.co/kgs/6vgLUu www.desireeholt.com www.desiremeonly.com
Follow me on BookBub https://www.bookbub.com/search?search=Desiree+Holt
Amazon https://www.amazon.com/Desiree-Holt/e/B003LD2Q3M/ref=sr_tc_2_0?qid=1505488204&sr=1-2-ent

Signup for my newsletter and receive a free book:
https://desireeholt.com/newsletter/

If you are not already a member of my reader group, Desiree's Darlings, please come and join me. Every day is a party.
https://www.facebook.com/groups/DesireesDarlings

Looking forward to "seeing" you there.
Desiree

AUTHOR NOTE

Heroes Rising

Prequels
Guarding Jenna
Unmasking Evil

Series
Desperate Deception
Zero Hour
Fatal Secrets
The Hunt

DEAR READERS,

When I started this series many titles ago, I just wanted to honor the SEALs, the U. S. Navy's primary Special Operations Force and a component of the Naval Special Warfare Command. SEALs are typically ordered to capture or to eliminate high level targets, or to gather intelligence behind enemy lines. They work in such highly intense situations that many times, when they leave the service, especially because being wounded affected their ability to do their jobs, there is a period of mental and emotional adjustment. But they still have so much to contribute and it's just a matter of finding the right fit for them. That's what Heroes Rising is about. Former SEAL Alex Rossi, the new sheriff in town, is having to rebuild his entire staff and he reaches out to—what else—former SEALs. And when Elle James invited me to write in her Brotherhood Protectors World I thought, what better place, since the man who created Brotherhood Protectors, Hank Patterson, is also a former SEAL.

The series actual began with two prequels, GUARDING JENNA and UNMASKING EVIL. If you haven't read them, then briefly, Jenna is back to her hometown in Montana in answer to a plea to find out who is raping and killing young girls.

Former SEAL Scot Nolan is hired to protect her. And yes, I left some threads dangling, as so many of you pointed out, but I had a reason. In UNMASKING EVIL, new sheriff Alex Rossi, in solving the murder of Micki Schroder's father, also solved the brutal riddle of the rapes.

But there were still some threads hanging out there, which is why I wrote THE HUNT. This book brings in Alex Rossi as well as characters from the earlier books: Zane Halstead and his wife, Lainie; Jesse Donovan and his fiancée, Teresa Fordice; and the head of Brotherhood Protectors himself, Hank Patterson.

I hope you enjoy this book and it answers everyone's questions.

Yours forever,
Desiree Holt
XOXO

CHAPTER 1

BRANTFORD "WOLF" Makalski rolled over in bed and punched the alarm off on his cell. He winced only slightly as the damaged muscles in his shoulder and upper arm protested the movement.

Better do those exercises.

Yeah, the damn exercises. But if he didn't... Problem was, he hadn't, for way too long. He couldn't seem to find the motivation for doing much of anything, as a matter of fact, except taking care of Bailey. Only when his arm and shoulder stiffened to the point where movement became a problem did he manage to kick himself in the ass and address the issue.

Both the doctor and the physical therapists told him, without exercising he might lose the use of his shoulder and arm by as much as 80 percent. If he followed the program, he might have residual stiffness and some limitations, but it would be a hell of a lot better. Now, he forced himself through the painful routine each day even as he asked himself, *What for?* It wasn't like the SEALs were going to take him back.

And there was the root of his problem. Being a SEAL defined him. Without that, he had no idea who the hell he was or what he should do. It hadn't been his choice to leave, so mentally he hadn't been prepared.

The touch of a wet nose on his face reminded him staying in bed wasn't actually doing that. He opened his eyes again and stared into Bailey's soulful ones.

"You miss it, too, right, boy?"

He ruffled the dog's fur on his head and stroked his ears.

The Belgian Malinois had been trained to sniff out explosives and was attached to Wolf's team. Lighter and leaner than German shepherds, the breed sported a compact frame, an advantage when tandem parachute jumping or rappelling, an intrinsic part of many SEAL missions. Their exceptional sense of smell makes them an optimal breed for detecting Improvised Explosive Devices (IEDs). Which was how they both ended up in this little house instead of with the rest of his team.

That last mission in Afghanistan had been FUBAR—fucked up beyond all repair. Both he and Bailey had been hurt badly enough to be medically discharged. Two damaged misfits, he remembered thinking. But the SEALs had helped him with Bailey's adoption and, when they were both deemed fit to travel, they headed back to Wisconsin. They were good company for each other. In fact, Bailey was about the only one Wolf was fit to be around, surly as he'd become. There was one problem, however: now what did they do with the rest of their lives?

When the dog nosed him again he sighed, swung his legs out of bed, and stood up. Grabbed his boxer briefs and yanked them on. Then he shuffled into the kitchen where he opened the back door to let Bailey out into the yard. What a stroke of luck this house turned out to be. He'd been reluctantly ready to settle for some uninspiring apartment, not having any plans that required a choice of location. But not everyone would take Bailey, and the dog needed a place to stretch his legs, especially the injured one.

Driving the streets of a modest neighborhood, he'd seen the For Rent sign in front of the little bungalow. It wasn't much, and it needed some loving care, but it had a very big yard. When he looked at it, he could already see Bailey romping in it, a little unsteady still on the injured leg.

Probably because the place was in such sad condition, the rent had been astonishingly low. His conscience had prodded him to at least do what he could to make the place presentable. But things like painting and mowing the yard were hell on his shoulder, which was what had prompted him to start the exercises in the first place.

He'd been here now for six months. Six months

where he'd done nothing but buy groceries and hang out with Bailey. At least he hadn't turned himself into an alcoholic. He knew he needed to find some focus for his life, but he had no idea what the hell that was. He hadn't even been with a woman for so long, he wondered if he'd just lost interest. No, he corrected himself, they wouldn't be interested in *him.* Not the way he was now.

He'd always wondered about guys like him who had medical discharges and why it took so long for most of them to find a new focus. Some of them never did. Now he knew the answer. It was like going from one planet to another and feeling like the alien intruder.

He'd splurged and bought himself one of those single-serving coffee machines, since he was such a caffeine addict. Now, as he waited for Bailey to tire himself out, he filled a mug and turned to carry it to the table. As he did, some of the hot liquid splashed onto his hand, and like that, *the scene* flashed into his mind.

They'd been sent to rescue two civilians who were prisoners in a Taliban facility. Two aid workers. They planned it out so carefully, had sneaked to get pictures of the house where they were being held, the area around it. How many guards were protecting the village and what else was going on in the street. Stealth was the word, and they were the best at it. Even Bailey, who would sniff for explosives, had been trained to walk silently.

But where there were supposed to be only two guards, there turned out to be five. And they had set explosives around the house where the aid workers were being kept. Bailey sniffed them out, but when he approached, he bumped an almost-invisible trip wire *Boom!* Something hot splashed on his hand and he was tossed backward, hitting his head against the wall. He was unconscious when his team got him the hell out of there. And, kudos to them, they got Bailey and the aid workers, too, leaving a bunch of dead terrorists in their place.

When he woke in the field hospital, it was to learn both he and Bailey were being airlifted to the new military hospital at Weilerbach, Germany. Bailey would be taken to a veterinary the military used, and they would both be treated for their injuries.

And then…

Wolf shook his head, trying not to let the memories overwhelm him the way they usually did. When he discovered his shoulder had been shredded, much like Bailey's hip, it had taken him months to be able to cope with it. To realize he'd no longer be a SEAL. And that Bailey was being retired as an official bomb-sniffer.

Physical therapy had been a bitch. Mostly because he'd spent nearly all of it feeling sorry for himself. But at least he made sure to work with Bailey every day, which was probably why he didn't lose his mind altogether.

But the same question plagued him every single

day: if he wasn't a SEAL anymore, then who was he? What was he supposed to do with his life?

He shook his head and swallowed a big gulp of coffee, barely noticing the way it burned his tongue. He'd turned into such a loser, something he'd never, ever expected to be. At least he'd recently started physical therapy again and was doing his exercises on a daily basis. But how did he get to the next chapter in his life? What did he do with himself?

Bailey came bounding up onto the porch and bumped the door with his nose. Wolf opened it and took a moment to hug what at that instant was his only friend, before letting him in and filling his food and water bowls. Okay, he'd do his exercises then take a shower and… And what?

Might as well do his morning workout. That took up a chunk of time. He went to grab his phone from the bedroom, although since he didn't get any calls, he had no idea in hell why he worried about not having it. As he picked it up, he saw a text had come in while he was in the kitchen. From Zane Halstead.

"Made a decision yet? Hope you decide to at least come and check us out. Just email me for details."

He'd been putting this off since he got the first text. And how the hell had this guy gotten his cell number? Probably through his military records, since he'd had to put it down when filling out the forms for his retirement and disability pay. Thank god no one else had tried to contact him, but these people must have some pull to access that information.

The first text had come in four weeks ago, and that he'd dismissed because…well, because. A few days later, he'd received another one, a couple of weeks later, a third. Why did these people want him in particular so badly?

Not that he'd seriously considered the offer , but it prompted him to at least get off his ass, do his PT every day on his shoulder, and find a gun range where he could train himself to shoot all over again. Luckily it had been his left shoulder, but having it out of commission affected his entire body. He was pretty happy with his progress so far, although he still had no clear goals in mind.

And then, today, a fourth text.

He stood there scrolling through the past messages. As he read through them, he felt like the biggest loser in the world. Okay, so he was used to having the ability to do anything, but he wasn't the only war vet who had challenges. Many of them were far worse off than he was, and he thought it entirely possible they were doing much better than he was.

Which was why he now was searching for the original message from Halstead. They'd gone through BUD/S together a lifetime ago, which was how they knew each other. And there it was. The first text.

"Thought of you for this. Tough to track you down though. And, oh yeah, the sheriff, Alex Rossi, is a former SEAL himself. He's new, cleaning house and filling the slots with former SEALs. If interested, text your email, and I'll send you all the details. Or you can call me at this number. Hope to hear from you."

Wolf sat on the bed, staring at the phone. Why was this decision so hard to make? If he hid away from everyone for too long, he'd turn into a withered mass of flesh and bone.

Just do it.

Bailey chose that moment to lumber into the room. He sat down at Wolf's feet and looked at him with an expression on his face that could only be described as plaintive. The Belgian Malinois is a special breed, tolerating both hot and cold weather. Kid-friendly and dog-friendly, easy to train were more reasons why they were the dog most SEAL teams prefer. His brown coat accented by black ears and snout gave him a distinctive look. And he was loyal and dedicated beyond belief.

"What do you think, guy?" Wolf rubbed the dog's snout. "Want to go on a field trip? Meet some new people?"

Bailey rubbed his snout against Wolf's thigh and made quiet little noises.

"Yeah, me, too, big guy. But we need to do something, or we're both going to dissolve into dust."

He set the phone down and left it on the nightstand while he went through the exercises the physical therapist gave him. Fire shot through the damaged muscles of his upper arm and shoulder but he persevered, sweating like a pig and cursing loudly. He at least had to be able to use a gun if he expected to be considered for this job offered to him. Or any other job, for that matter. His gun was as much a part of his body as the hand that held it, so this was a must, no matter how much it hurt.

Finally, when he'd reached the upper limit of his pain level, he quit.

In the bathroom, he took a good look at himself in the mirror and thought again about Zane Halstead's text. About what his life would be like if he stayed where he was or what might happen if he checked this out. His dark-brown hair was almost shoulder-length. He'd chopped it himself a few times with scissors, which was probably why it looked like a blind person had done it. Once a week, he sort of scraped his face, so some careful trim could give him a decent chin covering.

He'd have to clean up better if he decided to check out Halstead's offer. Maybe take a trip to the dreaded barbershop in town and hope nobody was too interested in his business. Questions, even friendly ones, gave him hives. Shaking his head, he stepped into the shower. Finally, showered and dressed, he went back to the kitchen, Bailey right at his heels. He carried a fresh mug of coffee to the back porch and sat in one of the chairs, Bailey next to him. Two swallows of coffee, a long breath, and he began to type the text.

Lacey Cooper pulled her car into the pump at the truck stop and turned off her engine. She needed gas and iced tea, and a lucky break. It was hotter than blazing hell outside, which meant her air-conditioning had been running full blast, so when she stepped out of the vehicle, the heat was like a lit candle running over her skin. Which surprised her because she'd read that the temp in this area of Montana never even passed ninety.

Tonight she'd take advantage of the pool at the campground where she was staying. Plus, sleeping in the tent, she always got the cool night breezes.

She'd taken enough pictures the past few days to plaster every wall in her house. Not that she knew what she was shooting, except for some great scenery, but she kept thinking somewhere in there was a clue as to where Heather and Trace had disappeared to. Oh, sure, people had seen them, but mostly they kept to themselves. The people in the offices at the campgrounds where they'd stayed said they'd asked for information about hiking trails but hadn't been specific about which ones.

Great. Just great.

I wonder if Heather is sleeping well. Comfortable. Someplace with Trace . If they're sleeping at all. Where in the hell are those two lovebirds anyway? If they're just off the grid, I might have to beat them with a broom, giving me heart failure like this.

Her sister, Heather, and her fiancé, Trace, had driven to the Crazy Mountains more than a week ago. They were huge camping fans and, in their research for interesting spots, had become fascinated with the Crazies. Lacey, a nature and wildlife photographer herself, was fascinated by the pictures they'd sent the first few days and wondered if she should make the trip herself. Maybe meet up with them for a few days.

She'd waited a couple of days to make sure she could do it and then texted Heather. When she didn't get a response, she tried calling. No answer. That's when she got worried. For twenty-four hours, she kept texting and calling. Finally, sick with fear, she called the police in the area, any departments that looked like they served the Crazies. They all told her the same thing: they didn't consider someone *missing* for seventy-two hours, and people got lost in those mountains a lot.

Why wasn't anyone interested in helping her?

Even search and rescue wasn't optimistic, echoing what law enforcement had said. And she had no starting point. They actually spent a day and a night looking in likely areas, checking caves, everything, but there was no trace of the couple at all.

She decided the only thing was to fly out there, rent a car, and start looking herself. So far, her luck was zero, and her fear grew every day.

When she found them, she was going to spend the first fifteen minutes blistering their hides. Didn't they realize she'd worry herself to death not hearing from them? After all, it had been a week. *A week!*

Again she'd talked to law enforcement but without much success. They all pointed out to her the vastness of the area.

"Without a starting point, I'd have people out there looking for months," each of them told her.

The sad part of it was she was falling in love with the area. She'd moved a lot in her life, after their parents passed away, but no place had really felt like home to her. Trace ran a tour guide business, which he once said he could run from anywhere, and Heather was an in-demand artist so not locked into anyplace. They'd even discussed the possibility of the three of them moving here if they liked it.

Now, she just wanted to find what was left of her damn family and go from there.

She cursed silently and steadily under her breath while she filled her tank before parking in front of the convenience store. She needed something cold and wet, and she needed it now. The store was semi-crowded. She made her way to where the drink machines and the refrigerator cases were and grabbed a couple bottles of iced tea.

As she stood in line to pay for them, she let her gaze roam casually over the crowd. It was easy to spot the ranchers in their jeans, work shirts, and boots. Others were also dressed casually, and she was sure some of them were tourists. No hunters yet. Fall season in the Crazies had not yet started.

Lacey was familiar with some of the area. She'd been taking shots for different magazines over the past couple of years. This was a beautiful area and easy to show off. She'd raved about it and mentioned once or twice that she wanted to get pictures to include in a coffee table book she was doing. That was probably why Heather and Trace had chosen it for this trip. They were dedicated campers, loved exploring, hiking, all the things that went with it.

But they also knew the importance of keeping in touch with people.

She'd checked three campgrounds already, with minimum success. They'd stayed at one of them for two nights but hadn't been back since then.

Of course, the Crazy Mountains covered a huge area and were almost completely surrounded by private lands. Huge ranches. There was a lot of wealth in the area, and the ranchers used it to fight any effort to change the status of their land. There weren't a lot of towns, either. A few big ones like Billings and Livingston and Bozeman. She'd gone through the arduous and lengthy process of checking all the motels and hotels in the area on the off chance Heather and Trace had decided not to sleep under the trees, but, as she expected, no dice.

Now she was concentrating on some tiny ones like Eagle Rock in the area where she was currently searching. Here, for the first time, she'd had some luck. The campground where she registered was the one where the couple had spent two nights.

"We were surprised when they left," the woman who checked her in told her. "Your sister raved about it. Said it was the nicest one they'd stayed at. But when I woke up the next morning their vehicle and all their stuff was gone. They must have left before the sun rose."

That was the first big trigger for Lacey. Although she'd never gone on trips with them, she knew her sister. Sneaking off before dawn wasn't her style. But there was no clue to where they'd gone when they left. They could be anywhere by this time. She'd decided to broaden her search area.

Someone had told her about Alex Rossi, the new sheriff of this county who was a former SEAL. Said those guys could find a gnat on the moon, and she should talk to him. Especially since the campground was in his area. She knew the reputation SEALs had. She figured if anyone could find them, it would be this sheriff.

She hadn't checked the area around Eagle Rock yet, so she had gotten directions to his office from the campground and planned for him to be her next stop. When she called, he'd told her he'd be there most of the afternoon.

She started toward the checkout counter, but a man stopped her.

"Miss Cooper?"

She looked at him and frowned. He was about five ten with graying black hair, thick brows, and deep-set eyes, and the kind of tan that came from spending a lot of time outdoors. How did he know who she was?

She frowned at him. "Do I know you?"

"Oh, sorry." He smiled. "I always think everyone knows me. Cordell Ritchie. President of the Crazy Mountains Ranchers Association. Been here a long time. I heard you were looking for your sister."

"Wow. Word must be getting around."

His smile was the kind people called polished. Well, if he had a political position, that made sense.

"We're a pretty spread out populated area," he told her, "but we try to keep a handle on what's going on and help where we can. I just want you to know that all the ranchers will be looking on their property to see if they can find anything. Including checking the parts of the mountains that bleed onto us."

Lacey managed a smile. "That's a very generous offer on your part, Mr. Ritchie."

He dipped his head. "We try to take care of each other." He took out his wallet and slid a thin business card from it, held it out to Lacey. "Call me any time. And how about giving me yours, in case we come up with anything. My ranch hands are out all the time, and they can certainly keep searching."

Well, she'd take all the help she could get, since other people weren't standing in line to offer it.

Lacey fished in her own wallet for one of her business cards, handing it over.

Ritchie studied it. "Wildlife photographer? Must be a great job."

"It is." She flashed a smile. "I really love my work. But it's also helped me with my search, because I look at places differently than other people do. I see things they don't."

"Let's hope it gets you some results. As warm as the days can be, the nights in the mountains can get pretty cold. I'm sure people have told you that disappearing in the Crazies is easy to happen, and the people are hard to find. There are so many caves and cracks and crevices that a search is always difficult. But we'll keep looking. I've passed the word to my hands and the association members to keep a sharp eye out."

Lacey forced a smile. "Well, thank you. I really appreciate it."

"No problem. You have my card if you need anything."

She wondered how he knew who she was. But of course, she'd been asking questions everywhere. A man in his position would certainly hear about it, she guessed. And maybe someone had given him a description. It was nice of him to offer, but something about him rubbed her the wrong way. Maybe it was his ego that he wore on his sleeve or his slightly condescending manner. She puzzled over it while she paid for her drinks and as she hurried out to her SUV.

After she cranked the ignition, she let the engine run for a few while the AC kicked on. Then she pulled out the directions to Alex Rossi's office and punched them into her GPS.

"Exit parking lot and turn left on highway. Then proceed ten miles."

She made the turn and headed down the paved two-lane road. Lodgepole pines crowded the edges and, beyond them, she could see stretches of land peppered with the same trees. She had just crested a small rise in the highway and made another turn when a bright flash of sunlight blinded her. She blinked, jerked the wheel, and struggled to bring the vehicle straight again. As another flash blinded her, she heard a loud noise, the sound of the driver's window shattering, and felt a sharp pain in her arm. The car slid to the right, and she was unable to hold it straight. The next thing she knew, it had slewed off the road, smashing into a thick lodgepole pine.

That was all she knew before falling into blackness.

CHAPTER 2

"We're almost there, buddy."

Wolf reached across the console and ruffled Bailey's fur. The dog had been an excellent traveler. The trip from Wisconsin had taken more than two days, driving at a normal pace. He hadn't wanted to hurry. For one thing, even though he'd agreed to come here and talk to Zane Halstead and his sheriff, he needed the time to get his shit together. From isolation to people was a big step. For another, he made regular stops for Bailey to get out and stretch his legs and take care of business. While he felt a thread of excitement at meeting these guys, it was tough pulling himself out of the zone of isolation where he had been comfortable for so long.

But he'd decided a fresh start needed something new. He had used some of his medical pension from the SEALs to treat himself to a brand-new pickup, fully tricked out. He hadn't done anything for himself for so long, he felt weird. Almost guilty. He kept telling himself he wasn't trying to impress anyone. But he also didn't want them to think he had turned into a useless bum. And it was for himself, too. Maybe if he stopped feeling sorry for himself, he could get back some self-respect.

He had just crested a small rise and followed a curve in the road when something on the right snagged his eyes and blinded him for a minute.

"What the fuck?"

He slammed on the brakes and pulled over to the shoulder until he got his bearings. He closed his eyes for a moment to clear his vison then opened them only to catch another burst through the lodgepole pines. There. What was it? He pulled the truck forward on the shoulder and put it in park.

"Hold on, buddy," he told Bailey. "I gotta check this out."

He made sure no cars were coming as he climbed out of his pickup and trudged toward the thicket of trees. When he saw what was there he blinked.

Holy fucking shit!

An SUV had somehow missed the turn and crashed into the trees. Wolf made his way carefully to where the vehicle's nose was kissing a thick tree trunk. The driver, a woman, was slumped over the wheel, nose into the airbag. He needed to check her for injuries, but when he tried the driver's side door, it was locked. Of course it was. Nobody drove around in this age of carjackings with their doors unlocked.

He looked around on the ground and smiled when he found some loose rocks lying there. Rocks, not little stones, thank the lord. Big enough for what he needed. He picked one up and, positioning himself so hopefully the glass would shatter away from the driver, he smashed the rock into the rear window. Because of his shoulder he had to use both hands, but he got it on the second try. The woman did not move at the sound, which was not a good sign.

Yanking his shirt up to cover his hand, he brushed away shards of glass so he could reach around and press the button to unlock her door. Finally, with his uninjured arm, he managed to drag the door open enough to check her...and discovered yet another problem. Blood streaked the woman's left arm and was still welling from what he knew was a bullet hole. And maybe with the bullet still in it.

What the fuck?

He stared at her for a long moment as something inside him turned over, some emotion he hadn't felt in a very long time. Since the disaster that left him with his injuries, he had not been able to connect emotionally with anyone, never mind a woman. But with this unknown woman, something inside him clicked open and feelings began to spill out.

What the hell?

Women hadn't played a role in his life since the medics dragged him out of the blown mission with part of his body in shreds. Not even a twitch in his cock. He'd begun to think he'd never want to have sex again, especially the meaningless kind that was his habit. Not even a dream that he could wake from and take his dick and his good right hand into the shower to take the edge off. So why, in this disastrous circumstance, did something about this woman reach deep inside him? How weird was that? He'd better pull up that famous SEAL self-control.

Her face, what he could see of it around the big now-crooked sunglasses and the curtain of rich auburn hair that had fallen forward, was so damn pale it scared him. She also had a bump on her forehead that he touched gently. He noticed how soft her skin was as he righted the sunglasses and brushed the hair back. He wanted to...

Forget what he wanted. This was a badly injured woman, and he could just shove his response to her in cold storage where it belonged. Where reactions like that had been for too fucking long, as a matter of fact. Maybe that was his problem.

But Jesus!

Pushing everything else away, he touched the tip of two fingers to her carotid artery, relieved to feel a pulse. He pulled a thankfully clean handkerchief from his pocket and wrapped it around the wound that was oozing blood.

What the hell was she doing out here, and who could have shot her? And why?

Okay, asshole, enough of that.

Right now, she needed medical attention, and he needed help getting her loose from the car. She was also partially blocked by the exploded airbag. Although he managed to push some of the fabric aside, he sure couldn't do it all himself. Damn fucking shoulder. Maybe this was a sign that the opportunity here in Montana was one he should accept. He'd already decided she needed protection, and he wanted to be the one to provide it.

Well, he'd better get his ass in gear and get this woman some help. He'd sure love to know, though, what someone like her had done to deserve being shot like this in the middle of nowhere.

Swallowing a sigh, he trudged back to his pickup where Bailey waited patiently in the shotgun seat.

"We got a problem, kiddo, and we have to ask for help. You guard the truck, okay? I'll just be right over there." He pointed to the wreck.

Bailey turned his head and stared at him with his soulful eyes, as if to say, "Now what?" He sat up on the seat, his eyes glued to Wolf, watching him as he went about trying to rescue this woman.

Wolf grabbed his cell phone from the holder in the console and scrolled through his contacts to where he'd stored Zane Halstead's number. What a great introduction, he thought. Taking a deep breath, he hit the Call icon and listened while it rang at the other end.

"Wolf?" It was answered on the second ring. "I

hope you're not calling to say you changed your mind."

"No, although you might not be so glad to hear from me when I tell you what's going on."

"Oh? What's the deal? Got a problem?"

"You could say. By my reckoning, I'm about two miles from your office. I've got a crashed car and an unconscious woman with a gunshot wound to the arm."

"Well, you sure do like to make an entrance. Are you east or west of us?"

"East."

"Be right there."

"Look for my truck," he told the man.

Disconnecting, he spoke a few settling words to Bailey who lay down on the seat again. Then he made his way back to the car. The woman still had not regained consciousness, which worried the hell out of him. He had learned some first aid in the SEALs, but he didn't think he should move her himself and possibly do more damage.

He had just checked her pulse when a soft moan drifted from her mouth.

Thank god, he thought.

"Hurts," she mumbled.

He bet it did.

"Don't move," he told her. "We'll have you out of here pretty quick and get you some medical attention."

"Camera," she whispered.

"What?" He leaned a little closer.

"My…camera."

Then he noticed what had to be a very, very expensive camera lying in the well of the passenger side. It had obviously fallen there when she slid off the road.

"Don't worry," he assured her. "I'll take care of it."

She seemed to be unconscious again, so he had no idea if she even heard him.

At that moment, he heard the approaching wail of a siren. Walking back up to the shoulder of the road, he saw a cream-colored SUV with a logo on the door pull over to the side, shut off the siren, and park. Two men climbed out. One of them, about six feet, had dark-brown hair that matched the scruff on his square jaw.

"What have we got?" he asked Wolf.

"Injured person. Female. Crash injuries plus a bullet wound in her arm."

"She's been shot? Damn. Is she conscious?"

Wolf shook his head. "Not at the moment."

"Let's take a look," the man behind them said. "I'm Alex Rossi. This is one of my deputies, Zane Halstead. The man who convinced you to come out here."

"Glad to see you made it even under the circumstances," Zane said. "We'll shake hands later."

"Yeah. I guess I sure know how to make an entrance."

Rossi was taller and leaner than Zane, with a hard

look on his face. Wolf at once sensed the presence of a former SEAL. All the Special Forces teams were incredible, but there was something about SEALs he believed set them apart. Maybe because of their motto: "The only easy day was yesterday." But even more than that, there was an invisible something that created an instant connection between members of the Teams. A connection that included trust.

Wolf watched as Alex climbed down to the car and leaned in to check on the woman.

"Glad to meet you. Okay if I call you Wolf?" One corner of his mouth quirked in a hint of a grin. "Hate to say it, but you don't look like a Brantford."

"No problem. I don't feel like one, either."

We don't usually welcome people quite like this. Zane says you brought us a little present."

"Yeah, came across her as I made the curve in the road. The sun glinting off either the glass or the metal from her car is what caught me. She's barely conscious, and I didn't want to move her until we got some medical help. Plus getting her out of the car in the first place is going to take some doing."

"Good move." Alex nodded. "I called right away for an ambulance just in case. It's on its way and should be here soon. Glad I did."

"Apparently it didn't have too far to come."

"There's a fire department substation in Eagle Rock with a fully staffed paramedic crew. Believe it or not, we get a fair number of accidents on ranches beyond the normal emergencies."

"Thanks for doing that. Seems she'll need it." Wolf gestured at the shattered glass. "Sorry for the mess, but I had to break a window to access the vehicle, and I opened the door to check on the victim. Do you know her?"

Alex frowned.

"No, she doesn't look familiar. Let's check for a purse as soon as we get her out of here." He managed to maneuver his arm through the smashed window, being careful of the glass, and reach for Lacey's wrist. "Low but not dangerously so."

The woman moaned again, tried to move, and cried out as pain shot through her.

"Hold on," Wolf told her, reaching for her uninjured hand. "Help is here."

Alex crouched next to her. "Can you tell us your name?"

She mumbled something indistinguishable, her words slurring.

"Sorry," he told her. "Can you manage to repeat that?"

"L—Lacey." Pain slashed across her face. "Cooper. Lacey Cooper."

Alex looked at Wolf, shock evident on his face.

"Lacey Cooper. Damn."

"I thought you didn't know her."

"I don't, but I had an appointment to meet with her today." He lowered his voice. "That's probably where she was heading when this happened. Her sister and the fiancé are here camping. They've gone missing, and she's rattling everyone's cage to look for them, without much success. It's really hard to do a search and rescue in the Crazy Mountains, and I guess, except for one attempt, people have blown her off. Maybe she was onto something after all."

"Yes. Need...help," she managed to say.

Alex crouched beside the open doorway of the SUV.

"Lacey, I'm Sheriff Rossi. I sure didn't expect us to meet like this but, I promise you, I definitely want to hear what you have to say."

"May...be...running out of time." She managed to get the words out in a voice laced with pain.

"We'll get it under control," he assured her. "But let's get you taken care of first."

"Camera," she said again.

"She's got what looks to be a damn expensive camera lying on the floor there. We ought to get it and bring it with us."

Alex nodded. "As soon as she's out of here."

"What can I do?" Wolf wanted to know.

"I need the jaws of life to do this." He turned to head back to his vehicle. "I don't want to wait until the paramedics get here."

But Zane was already there, carrying the big instrument, and the wail of another siren sounded at the same time. Then the paramedics were there with their equipment and a stretcher, the door had been removed, and the airbag cut away. The paramedics took care of the seat belt, holding the woman so she wouldn't fall forward, and being careful with her arm.

"That's a bullet wound," one of them told Alex.

"I figured. I've for sure seen enough of them."

"And the bullet's still in there. We'll pack the wound until they can remove it."

"Hurts," Lacey mumbled again as she tried to shift in her seat.

"Just hold on," one of the paramedics told her. "We're moving you to a stretcher right now and then we can help with that pain."

Wolf stood to the side, out of everyone's way, but he was unable to take his eyes from Lacey Cooper's injured body. There was something about her that touched places inside him that had been in the deep freeze for a very long time. She looked tough and vulnerable at the same time. Who the fuck had shot her? And why? Every muscle in his body was tense as he watched the paramedics take her vital signs, reciting them to whatever medical facility was on the other end of the radio. Then they placed an oxygen mask over her face and adjusted the flow.

Their two-way radio crackled with conversation as they sent information and asked questions. Finally they gave her a shot of the pain meds the hospital had okayed and eased her onto a stretcher.

"She's got a bump the size of a tomato on her head," one of the paramedics told Alex Rossi. "They'll x-ray her and do a complete physical at the hospital before they take her into surgery for that bullet wound."

"You're taking her to Livingston, right?" Zane asked.

"Yes, sir. Should I let them know you'll be along?"

"Actually, Deputy Halstead will follow you. I want to go over the car here and then I have a meeting with Mr. Makalski."

"Hey." Wolf raised his hand. "We can put that off while you handle this. No problem."

Alex shook his head. "Not a problem. In fact, this will give you a good chance to see how we work." His mouth quirked in a tight grin. "Tell the doctors she will be under guard at all times."

"They won't let him in the operating room," he reminded the sheriff.

"I know, but he can watch from the observation room. After seeing this, even before speaking with her, I'm not leaving her unguarded." He handed the man his card. "If anyone has a problem, they can call me."

Wolf stood by silently while the paramedics loaded Lacey Cooper into the ambulance.

"Don't let her out of your sight for a minute," Alex told Zane in a low voice.

"Got it. No problem."

Seconds later, the ambulance hit the highway, siren wailing, Zane Halstead following them.

Alex Rossi heaved a sigh and turned to Wolf. "Not exactly the way I planned for our first meeting to go."

"One thing I learned in the SEALs," Wolf told him, "is that you should always be prepared to expect the unexpected."

Rossi barked a laugh. "Yeah, I think it's endemic in the SEALs. I assume that's your truck over there? Nice set of wheels."

"The one I had was a piece of junk, just like I was turning my life into. Figured I'd start a new life with new wheels." His mouth curved in a half grin. "I might have gone a little overboard."

"Is that a dog I see?" Alex squinted his eyes against the sun.

"That's Bailey. He was our bomb sniffer on my team. He and I were both casualties of our last mission." He frowned. "Is that going to be a problem?"

Alex grinned. "Not at all. We'll have to introduce him to Six."

"Six?" Wolf frowned. "Is that a person?"

"A dog," the sheriff told him. "A German shepherd, also a veteran like your Bailey. His owner, Kujo—"

"Wait." Wolf held up a hand. "Kujo? Should I be afraid?"

Alex managed another tiny grin. "Joseph Kuntz, but everyone knows him as Kujo. He and Six work as a team for Brotherhood Protectors, so you can see this is nothing new for us. We'll have to get you guys together."

"That would be good. I'd like to meet him."

"We'll definitely arrange it." Alex rubbed his jaw.

"Well, I could get on the radio and put out a call for one of my deputies to help analyze this scene, but I have a feeling you'd be a good substitute. You okay with this?"

"Sure. Lead on."

Wolf wasn't even sure yet if he wanted the job, or if Alex Rossi would decide to offer it to him. Or even if he wanted to move to Montana, although he'd finally realized he needed to make some kind of change before he just turned into dust. And bitter dust at that. Still, he figured this was as good a way as any to find out if he was up for it and if he and Rossi could work together.

First order of business was checking out the car. They found the woman's purse jammed beneath the passenger seat. Alex yanked it out and opened it, finding her wallet.

He trailed as the sheriff walked back along the edge of the road, following the skid marks of Lacey Cooper's car. They found the exact spot her car had jerked and slid onto the shoulder.

"It's hard to tell for sure," Rossi told him, "but it looks like this is the spot where she was hit—"

He stopped and scanned the area.

Wolf did the same.

"Her left arm was hit, so the shot came from over there." He pointed to the left side of the road and the stands of lodgepole pines so thick, he could barely see anything beyond them.

"To make it work," Rossi said, "whoever did this

would have to be either up in one of the trees or on horseback. A car parked at the side of the road would be too obvious. If Lacey saw it, she might think someone was in trouble and stop to help. He couldn't just shoot her. Someone might come along while that was happening."

Wolf quirked an eyebrow. "I'm assuming most of the people around here ride?"

Rossi nodded. "A good many of them. Most of the land around the Crazy Mountains is privately owned and contains large ranches anywhere from hundreds to thousands of acres."

"So, a lot of rich people, too."

"Yes. They kind of have their own community and make their own laws. Not all of them but the top dogs. Before I took over as sheriff, the man who held the position looked the other way while a group of them raped underage girls as a hobby."

Nausea washed up in Wolf's mouth. "Are you shitting me?"

"Not even a little. They paid off the previous sheriff to look the other way. What was worse, if any of the girls reported it, he passed that along, and the girl was killed."

"Jesus." Wolf didn't know what to say. Just the thought of it disgusted him.

"Yeah, solving it and cleaning up the mess was my first project when I was hired." He gave a short, bitter laugh. "Of course, I had to fire almost every deputy to get it done."

Wolf stared. "You mean, they were all in on it?"

"One way or another. For money, of course. But I'm building a great staff, which is what we'll be discussing as soon as we see what's what today. Anyway, back to your question. Yes, most of the population of this county rides, at least enough to get around."

"So someone could have ridden up here, hidden the horse in the trees, climbed one of the pines—or not—and taken the shot."

"You got it." He rubbed his jaw. "The thing is, it would have to be someone who was either tracking her or knew she was coming to see me today. Of course, her reason for being here isn't exactly secret."

"Oh?"

"Her sister and her fiancé have been camping in the Crazies and apparently having a great time, until, that is, they just disappeared."

Wolf blinked. "Disappeared?"

"Yeah." Alex sighed. "She's been asking questions and trying to get some help. Problem is, people have disappeared in the Crazies before and, unless it's in some familiar or easily accessible cave, most of them never get found. This is still pretty much a wilderness area, and the Crazies are filled with caves and other hidey holes."

"But she was coming to see you," Wolf reminded him.

Alex gave a short laugh. "My undeserved reputation precedes me. My deputies and I were able to find and rescue a couple of people over the past couple of years. Trust me, though, it was more luck than brains."

"Maybe it's because none of the others were SEALs," Wolf joked.

"Best explanation yet. Anyway, let's see if we can find anything on this side of the road. Then I'll get pictures of the car and surrounding area. We also need to retrieve her camera and her purse and anything else she left in it. But first I'm calling the towing service. It'll take them a while to get here."

Wolf helped Alex measure the skid marks of Lacey's car, which gave them an idea of where the shot had entered her vehicle. Then he helped him check the entire car, waited while the sheriff snapped pictures inside and out and from all angles. Finally, they crossed the road and tried to find something in the thick stand of pines.

"Well, that was pretty much a waste of time. The pine needles were stirred, but it could have been a breeze or wild animals, not necessarily someone hiding there on a horse." Alex stored all the equipment he'd used in his SUV. At that moment, his cell rang, and he pressed the button to answer. "How's it going? Yeah? Yeah? Okay. Hang tight. We'll be on our way as soon as the tow truck gets here for the car. But call me if anything changes or anything suspicious turns up in the meantime. Thanks."

"Report from the hospital?" Wolf couldn't help asking.

Alex nodded. "They're just prepping her for surgery now. The doctor wanted X-rays first and lab work."

"Did she wake up?"

"Just barely. Zane says she's got a slight concussion and some swelling on the brain, which is so not good."

Wolf felt sick, and he didn't even know the woman, although he damn sure wanted to. "Do they have to operate to relieve the swelling, too?"

Alex shook his head. "No. At least not at the moment. And they made sure she was okay for the surgery on her arm. Here comes the tow truck. As soon as he's done, we can head to my office and have our discussion. Let's take care of our business and then I'm off to Livingston."

"Listen." Wolf cleared his throat. "If you don't mind, I'd kind of like to ride to Livingston with you. I found her, so I have kind of a vested interest. And we can talk on the way." He paused. "If that's okay with you, I mean."

There was no doubt about that. Lacey Cooper was the first person to make him feel anything but pain and bitterness in a long time. Maybe she'd need a bodyguard and Alex Rossi would decide this would be a good test of Wolf's skills and commitment. He just hoped he'd be up to it. That meant he *really* needed to have his shit together.

Alex studied him a moment before he nodded. "Sure. That works. I can have your truck delivered to the house I told you about and pick both of you up at the hospital when Lacey is discharged. But what about your dog? We can take him with us, but will he wait in your truck all the time you're at the hospital?"

Wolf looked back at the dog. Bailey was good to stand on duty for a long time, but he wasn't too anxious to lock him in the truck for an extended period.

"Yeah, I need to figure that out." He scratched his head, torn by the need to be in two places at once.

"Let me call Kujo." He pulled out his cell. "He might have a solution."

Wolf rubbed his jaw. "I'm not too anxious to just hand him over to someone else."

"Kujo's not just anyone. Like I said, let me make the call. I bet he has a solution." He speed-dialed a number and walked away while he talked. Wolf figured if it turned out to be a problem, he wanted to keep the conversation private. But when he walked back, he was grinning.

"Well?" Wolf asked.

"Told ya. Kujo and Six will meet us at the hospital, and we'll see if what I proposed works. We won't do anything to stress Bailey out. Now, let me touch base with the tow truck driver. As you can see, he's got one of those big flatbed haulers. We can have him drop your truck off at my office and then get going. Give me your keys, and I'll hand them over with Lacey's."

Wolf felt naked without his truck keys, but he

figured Alex Rossi didn't need to waste the time detouring to his office just to drop a vehicle.

He checked the inside of his truck, taking a moment to reassure Bailey, and stopping when he came to the gun in its holster in the console. He lifted it out and looked at Alex.

"I'm not licensed to carry here. I don't want to cause a problem, but I sure feel naked without this."

"Not a problem. I'll handle it if anything comes up. I know what you mean, so just bring it with you. But you won't be able to bring it into the hospital."

"Understood. I guess that goes for the rifle, too."

"Sorry." Alex flashed a brief grin. "SEALs feel naked without their weapons, right?"

"Absolutely."

"I'll bring it to the house and have it waiting there for you. Okay, then, why don't you let Bailey have a pit stop and then we'll get to it. I'll fill you in on what we're looking for and hopefully we can come to an agreement."

"Just like that?"

"Like I said, you're a former SEAL. That's good enough for me. Let's get moving."

CHAPTER 3

"It's starting to get dark again. And cool."

They'd chosen this time of year to visit the Crazy Mountains because the days were warm but not hot and the nights pleasantly cool. They hadn't expected to be spending the nights outside with little protection, running for their lives.

Heather stood with her arms wrapped around herself. The thin jacket offered little protection against the chill of the night but she was glad she'd been wearing it when they were grabbed. She wished she'd been wearing jeans instead of shorts. Her legs wouldn't be so badly scraped from the gnarly bushes and trees. Trace had his sweatshirt on, another lucky break. Without those coverings, meager as they were, they could easily freeze to death.

Through the chinks in the logs of the walls of the shack, she could see the sun beginning to set. Soon, the man would bring them their meager food, enough to keep them alive and able to play their dangerous game.

"What's the fun in it if you're too weak to play?" he joked frequently. "The longer we can make it last, the bigger the bet."

"You bet on this?" Trace had been as shocked by that as he was by the "game" itself.

"Sure. We've been betting on hunts since we got our first guns. But humans make much better prey than animals. More of a challenge."

The challenge for her and Trace had been staying alive. She still had trouble believing this was happening. One minute, they were getting a personal tour on a local ranch because that was on Trace's list. Hers, too. She thought she'd get great photos. The next minute, they felt they'd been stung by a bee.

Except they got dizzy immediately. They woke up in this very crude one-room cabin, disoriented and having no idea what the hell was going on.

When they learned the answer, panic didn't begin to describe what they felt.

The man—"Call me Hunter."— (and wasn't that just the most appropriate name for him) was standing in the one-room shack, watching them as they woke up from the drugs on the darts they'd been struck with. Trace was already trying to shake it off when she managed to open her eyes and sit up. Her head pounded, and she was afraid she was going to throw up. When she saw the hooded man standing there, fear raced through her body and froze her in place.

"Who—Who are you?" she asked.

"I already asked," Trace told her. "You won't like the answer."

She turned back to the man. Hunter.

"Where are we? Why are we here? People will be looking for us."

His laugh sent chills racing through her.

"People disappear in the Crazies all the time. Many of them never get found. You two will just be added to that list."

"Nope." Trace pushed himself to his feet, albeit a little unsteady. "Not the people we know. They'll never give up."

Hunter laughed again. "We'll see. So. I've brought you some food. I suggest you eat it. You'll need your strength."

"For what?" She tightened her hands into fists to keep from shaking.

"A little game we like to play, my friend and I."

Trace stood in front of the man. "We didn't come out here to play games. I don't know what your game is, but we want out of here right now."

"If you earn it, freedom is yours." He pointed to a tray set on a crude table. "I suggest you eat something so you have plenty of stamina. You'll need it. I'll be back after dark with the rules."

He turned toward the door.

"Wait!"

Trace grabbed Hunter's arm. "Wait. You can't just leave us here like this."

Hunter one-armed him away, a mean look settling on his features.

"Now, that's where you're wrong. I can do anything I want. Eat and rest. You'll need your strength. We'll see how long you last."

He pulled the door open and slammed it shut behind him. Heather heard a heavy clicking sound.

"He latched it," Trace told her. "What the fuck is going on here?"

"I'm scared." Heather threw her arms around him and pressed her body tight to his.

"I'm not too happy myself." He rubbed her back. "But I'll figure a way out of this. They must want to keep us alive. There's two sleeping bags over there, and he brought us food."

"Yes, but for how long?"

"We have to be smart, babe. As soon as we know what this is all about, we can figure a way out of it. I promise."

But that was before they knew the rules of The Hunt, which had been spelled out very carefully for them that first night.

"Run. Run as fast as you can. We'll let you do it together tonight since the game is just beginning. And hide. Avoid my partner and me. If you make it through the night without getting shot, you get to live another day."

She remembered how sick with fear she'd been, and how Trace had taken her hand and squeezed it.

"We can do this," he'd whispered.

Once they were out in the open, the first thing they'd done was look for a way off the property. But no matter where they ran—and there was a lot of land to cover—they came up against a chain-link fence with barbed wire on the top. And the links had been set with the rough edges facing in toward the property, so it was impossible to get a handhold. It had taken everything she had not to cry that night.

They'd tried again to find an escape the next night and the next, but everyplace they looked it was the same.

She'd been terrified that first night, running through stands of trees and thickets of wild underbrush, doing her best to avoid banging into a tree or having the bushes tear at her skin. The only thing that kept her sane was having Trace with her.

But as soon as it started to turn light, they managed to find their way back to the cabin. Hunter and his partner had been standing there, looking disappointed but still smiling.

"Well, well, well. You might prove to be worthy prey after all. Better get some rest before tonight."

The next night and the next had been the same, running and hiding even as they kept looking for a way out. God, maybe they'd survive this and be set free after all. At that moment, Heather heard the snick of the lock and the rasp of the bolt being moved. Then the door swung open and Hunter stood in the opening in his usual jeans, dark shirt, and the ever-present hood over his head.

Heather tasted the fear that surged in her throat the way it always did when he arrived to start the night's activities.

"Time to play, kids. Up and at 'em."

"If we win tonight, will you finally let us go?" She hated asking, but there had to be an end to this. Otherwise, one way or another, game or not, she was sure they'd be dead. Hunter had dropped little hints. Like the others who'd been kidnapped into this game had never been found.

"We'll see." He laughed again. "Maybe this'll be your lucky night. Let's go. We added a couple of rules."

She didn't think it was possible to be any more afraid than she already was, but at his words, her stomach clenched and she nearly vomited.

"What rules?" Trace asked. "Aren't there enough?"

"You guys are just smarter than we thought," Hunter told them. "We had to up the game a little."

"Like how?"

"So far, we've let you compete as a couple, but—"

"Compete?" Trace interrupted. "You call this a competition? You two have the guns, and we have nothing. That's no contest."

"You have your brains. And damned good ones, I might add. Best we've had yet."

They knew by this time there had been others.

Some singles, some couples. None had beaten the hunters.

"Well. Let's get to it." Hunter gestured with the rifle. "Outside. Now."

Trace took Heather's hand and gave it a squeeze as they walked out of the one-room cabin. The building sat in a little clearing, surrounded by thick stands of lodgepole pines that stretched forever. They knew from the previous nights that wild animals such as gray wolves, coyotes, and grizzlies roamed the area, along with elk, moose, and white-tailed deer. A variety of birds lived in the trees, and she and Trace had gotten used to hearing their calls. Although he had pointed out to her that some of those sounds could be Hunter and his friend mimicking the birds to communicate with each other.

It was black as pitch, with only a quarter moon hanging in the sky and the stars barely twinkling. A light breeze stirred the night air, adding to the chill factor. When they were standing just outside, Hunter walked around in front of them.

"Okay. Here's the rules for tonight. You each go in separate directions. I'll be hunting you, sweet thing." He nodded at Heather. "My partner's after your boyfriend. If you both make it back here okay, well, you get to hang around for another day."

"Are you ever going to let us go?" Heather cried.

Hunter shrugged. "I guess we'll have to think up a real challenge for that to happen. Now get going. My partner's already out there." When they didn't move, he shouted, "Haul ass."

Trace pulled Heather close to him, wrapping his arms around her.

"We can do it, babe. We've done it before."

"I'm so tired," she whispered. "Will he ever let us go?"

"I keep looking to see if there's a way out of here. Haven't found it yet, but there has to be. I'm not giving up."

"I love you." She pressed her face against him.

"Love you, too. Now, let's beat this thing."

"Cut the whispering," Hunter ordered, "or the game ends now."

Trace let go of Heather's hand and gave her a little nudge, and they took off running in opposite directions.

She had to weave in and around the trees, doing her best not to brush against the thin, scaly bark and to be careful of the accumulation of fallen pine needles and cones. That first night, she'd learned just how dangerous they could be.

Nothing happened for the first five or ten minutes. Then she heard the call of a bird she was sure was one of the men. She put on a burst of speed and, when she thought she was far enough away, she stopped to catch her breath.

Please, please, don't let them be near me.

As she leaned against a tree, bent over, drawing air into her lungs, two sounds sent a chill through her. The crack of a rifle and the bark of a wolf. She'd learned over the past few nights that wolves barked when they were near their prey. God! She forced herself not to panic and to stay absolutely still. But then she heard another shot, panic gripped her, and she took off.

She just had to stay out of sight until sunrise and be back at the cabin by then.

That's all. Just avoid getting shot to death or ripped apart by wild animals. Sure. Nothing to it.

God. Please let Trace be safe.

～

"Well, I don't usually conduct interviews in a car," Alex told him as they ate up the miles on the highway on the way to Livingston, "but this gives us a good chance to talk."

"Let me have it," Wolf told him.

They fell into a surprisingly comfortable conversation, interrupted only when Alex received a text message. He pulled over to look at it and smiled.

"Kujo likes the idea of the dogs. Let's see if it works."

When they reached the hospital, Alex stopped for a moment to send a text message, read the answer, and drove to the far side of the parking lot. He pulled up next to a pickup almost as tricked out as Wolf's.

"Think Bailey's ready to make a friend?"

"Let's give it a try," Wolf said.

He climbed out of the vehicle, snapped Bailey's leash on, and led the dog out of the car. By that time, the man he assumed was Kujo was also out of his truck with a large German shepherd sitting obediently beside him.

Alex introduced the two men, who nodded at each other, keeping their dogs a safe distance apart. Wolf and Kujo decided on how to do this and, before fifteen minutes had passed, the dogs were sitting patiently side by side as if to say, "What's next?"

Wolf felt relief surge through him. If this hadn't worked, he wasn't sure how he'd take this job.

"I don't even know how to thank you," Wolf told him.

Kujo shrugged. "SEALs stick together, right? Let me know what the arrangements are so I can set it up for you and Bailey to have a get-together once a day. Oh, and I looked up how Belgian Malinois received their commands and printed out the page."

Wolf was astounded and didn't know how to express his gratitude. But Kujo was right about the SEALs. For the first time since the discharge, he felt as if he had a life in front of him. He owed Zane Halstead more than a simple thanks.

He knelt down beside Bailey, rubbing the dog's face and ears then held his face between his palms.

"This is a new friend, Bailey. *Friend.* He is a good person and has a dog you can play with. Be nice and friendly." He rubbed the dog's ears again. "Behave, okay?"

Bailey gave a short, soft bark and licked Wolf's nose.

"I guess he's good with it." Wolf laughed and handed over the leash to Kujo. "Thanks again for this."

"Like I said, happy to do it."

"Molly okay with this?" Alex asked. He glanced at Wolf. "Molly's Kujo's wife. I think Six loves her better than he does Kujo."

Kujo laughed. "You got that right. Yes, we discussed it and she said if Bailey is anything like Kujo, she's happy to do it. Wolf, fill me in on him."

After fifteen minutes of the dogs analyzing each other, Kujo smiled.

"Okay," he said to Wolf. "We're good to go." He fished a card from his wallet and handed it to Wolf. "My cell and also the number for the Brotherhood Protectors office if you need it."

"Stop poaching my territory," Alex joked. "He came here to be one of my deputies."

Kujo held up both of his hands. "Just passing information."

Wolf spent another couple of minutes whispering to Bailey. Then he gave Kujo the basic information he'd need, thanked him again, and the men all shook hands. Wolf grabbed Lacey's camera and purse out of Alex's vehicle, and the two of them headed into the hospital.

"I know Zane's with the woman now," Wolf

commented, "but when we get to wherever she is, you can let him know I'm now on duty."

"I'll ask you again. You sure about this? You just spent a couple of days driving and—"

"No problem. I can always catch a few minutes in the chair in her room. And having Bailey taken care of covers a huge obstacle."

"Then, let's find out how she is."

Zane had called with an update as they drove to Livingston. Lacey was out of surgery for the bullet, so after riding up in the elevator, they knew just where to go. They passed through a set of doors and turned into a large room with beds surrounded by curtains.

"Zane texted that she's still in recovery," Alex told him.

After three surgeries himself, Wolf certainly knew about the recovery ward. Unpleasant memories assaulted him, and again he had to steel himself to move forward. The moment they stepped inside the area, a nurse in surgical garb hurried over to them.

"I'm sorry, but you can't be in here," she said.

"I just need to check with my deputy," Alex told her. "He was sent here by me to stand guard because the patient is in some danger."

"So he said when he walked in." She frowned. "I can't have strangers cluttering up this room. It's for postsurgical patients."

"He texted me that the hospital director okayed it." Alex's tone was pure patience.

"That's what I heard." A tiny smile quirked one corner of the nurse's mouth. "If I didn't know Zane's wife so well, I'd have thrown him out of here."

Wolf fought a grin. Small-town politics everywhere. Everyone had their own territory.

"I understand," Alex agreed. "But she's in protective custody, and I just need a minute to check on her. Also, I need to set my deputy here up since he'll be taking over guard duty. Then I'll get out of your hair."

"Fine, but make it quick."

"Zane's wife volunteers at the hospital twice a week," Alex told Wolf. "Let's go. Zane's motioning us to come over to the bed where he's standing."

"She did well in the surgery," he told them in a low voice. "There is some swelling on the brain, but they're treating it with medication and lowering the body temperature."

"All that with the accident and surgery from the bullet wound." Alex shook his head. "Been there, done that." He looked at the other men. "We all have."

"The doc says she's very strong," Zane told them. "She should make a full recovery. But we can't leave her alone. Whoever did this will sniff around and find out she's not dead and try to take another run at her."

"She must be some woman." Alex rubbed his jaw. "Apparently she's been rattling cages around here for more than two weeks, driving everyone nuts when she didn't get any answers. And she's not shy about who she speaks to. I asked around, and I'll tell you, if anything ever happens to you, this is who you want digging for answers."

"Well, apparently she rattled the wrong cage," Zane pointed out. "I'd give a bundle to know whose it was, because this takes it out of the lost hikers and into another more dangerous area."

"Sure does," Alex agreed. "It puts it into a whole different category. We're not just looking for lost campers here. There's obviously someone out there with something to hide about this who wasn't shy about taking a shot at her."

"We need to figure this out," Zane added. "Before they go after her again."

Alex nodded. "Let's step out in the hall for a minute."

"But..." Wolf gestured at Lacey, so pale in the hospital bed.

"I'll get the nurse to watch her for a bit," Zane told them. "This won't take long." Once they were out in the hall, he turned to Wolf. "I bet you didn't quite expect your welcome to go this way. Hope it doesn't chase you off."

"Actually, I kind of feel as if I have a vested interest in her. I mean, after finding her in the car and all. And it feels good to be useful again."

"I get that all right. At first I thought about reaching out to Hank Patterson for one of his guys, but—"

"Who's Hank Patterson?" And what made him better?

"He runs a private security operation here in Eagle Rock called Brotherhood Protectors. They're all SEALs, too."

"It's like an epidemic around here." Zane winked.

Alex laughed. "Of the good kind. But, Wolf? That was an excellent conversation we had on the way here. Enough for me to hire you as Lacey's bodyguard. Plus, I had already checked your records before Zane even called you. Top drawer stuff. So, how about we call this a tryout."

Wolf glanced over at the sheriff. "A tryout?"

"Yeah. See how it works with you as Lacey's bodyguard until this all gets sorted out. Give you a chance to see if you like this place. And me and my guys. Then we can both make a decision about going forward. I think you'd be a good fit as one of my deputies, but all of this was really just dumped on you, so I want you to kind of test the waters. Does that work for you?"

Wolf definitely wanted the job. He'd realized that the minute he found Lacey in her car. There was this unexpected and unexplainable attachment he felt for her. He had no idea what was drawing him to this woman, but he wanted this job and he wanted to get to know her when she wasn't injured, so he nodded his agreement.

"I'm good. I can handle it. Do you know much

about her? Does she have family that needs to be notified?"

Alex shook his head. "I know very little about her except that she's a wildlife photographer and her sister is her only relative."

"So, strong and independent," he guessed.

"That's my impression," Alex agreed.

"I should be prepared for pushback?"

Alex chuckled. "My guess is as long as she gets her own way she's fine. Getting her to accept help is going to be a little touchy, but I get the impression you can handle it."

"SEALs are tough," he joked, amazed a sense of humor seemed to be coming back.

"Good, good. Now, uh, here's the thing I didn't mention. I don't have much of a slush fund in my budget, so the pay for this will be strictly minimal."

Wolf shook his head. "Money's not an issue. I've hardly spent a dime in the past six months. And if you're good with it, I'd really like to do this."

"Okay. Then we need to get back in there. I need to get you to Lacey and introduce you to the nurse taking care of her." Alex grinned. "She's a pistol all right. So, let's get you set up. I don't like leaving her this long, even in a part of the hospital that's pretty well protected, what with all the medical personnel around."

"It would be good," Wolf told him, "if we could talk to the doctor to see how long they expect her to be here and what her prognosis is."

Alex nodded. "I'll see if someone can find him for us."

Wolf realized there was so much he didn't know about this situation, and he passed that along to Alex now as they walked back into recovery.

"I'd like to know why she's been looking for her sister and the sister's fiancé in the first place. If they're missing, how long has it been since she's heard from them? Did she get any kind of answers the places she'd looked?"

"I'm with you there," the sheriff told him. "I actually know very little. I expected to learn that when I met with her today. I do, however, have people I can ask to fill in some of the blanks. Also, there's a receipt from one of the campgrounds in the area in her purse. I'll send someone over to check if she's still registered there. If so, we'll collect her stuff."

He and Alex hunted up the doctor who brought them up to date.

"The bump on the head is pretty big, but there was no damage to the brain," he told them. "Just some slight swelling which I'm pretty sure will go down quickly. "She has a slight concussion, which is the only reason we're keeping her overnight. The bullet wound could have been a lot worse than it was. We didn't have to do much digging. She'll be sore for a few days and won't have a lot of use of that arm at first, but she should heal nicely."

Wolf breathed a sigh of relief. He didn't even know Lacey Cooper, and already he was emotionally invested in her. That shocked the hell out of him, and he'd have to figure out why he felt this way. Meanwhile, he'd make damn sure no one got close enough to do her any more harm.

"I guess we'll have to say a lot of prayers," Alex said. "Okay. We don't have any of the background, although I might have a faint idea. Anyway, the important thing is to keep her safe, so we're going to have her under guard twenty-four seven."

"Good idea," the doctor agreed. "I assume you'll have someone in the room with her?"

Alex pointed to Wolf. "Meet Wolf Makalski. He'll be glued to her at all times. You know what I mean."

The doctor's mouth twitched in a faint grin. "Okay. Then I'll make sure the chair in the room we take her to is one of those recliners so he can catch a few winks now and then."

"Thanks very much." Alex turned to Wolf. "Go tell Zane he's relieved and I have an errand for him to run. Text me your cell number. I know Zane has it, but I need it, too. I'll send you mine and then we'll be good to go. Be sure to check in regularly."

Wolf was used to the process when they were assigned a new commanding officer. *You know your job. Do it and report regularly.*

"I'm on it," he assured the sheriff.

"You've got Lacey Cooper's purse and camera. Take charge of them until she gets moved into a room. Then you can stash them in the locker there."

"If it's all the same to you, I'll just hang onto them.

Never know who might be going through her things. I learned a long time ago that the people who appear the most trustworthy often aren't."

Alex grinned. "I think you might end up being a good addition to my staff. Okay, gotta run, but I'll check back with you."

Someone had brushed Lacey's hair back from her face, and she looked so pale and still. Her upper left arm was bandaged and immobilized across her chest in a sling. Wolf looked down at her and was swamped by a sudden overwhelming desire to keep her from harm. More than the usual need to protect that SEALs had etched in their DNA. There was something about her that reached out to him. Again, he wondered what it was about this woman that was unlocking parts of him locked away for so long. He swore to himself that no harm would come to her while she was under his care.

The same nurse as before appeared next to the bed. She was pushing a chair to give him something to sit on. "Standing for a long time is bad for the joints. By the way, my name's Natalie."

"Wolf Makalski." Wolf swallowed a smile and held out his hand.

The nurse shook it. "Nice to meet you, Wolf. Interesting name."

"My SEAL Teams code name."

"Oh? Any particular reason for that?"

Wolf was always embarrassed explaining it. His team leader said it honored his powerful instinct, intuition, and high intelligence. But telling people that made him uncomfortable.

"Probably because I have good hunting instincts for the enemy. Anyway, thanks for taking such good care of her."

She shrugged. "It's what I do. I heard she's looking for her sister?"

Wolf studied her face. "How did you know that?"

"Word travels. She's been asking different places where I know some people." She shook her head. "Damn shame, but those Crazy Mountains swallow people up like sinkholes."

That may be, Wolf thought, but he'd seen people disappear before, and nature had nothing to do with it. He was determined, however, to help Lacey Cooper find her sister and keep her safe while doing it. In a few short hours, Fate had changed his life, and he was going with it.

"They don't want her flinging that arm around," Natalie told him. "That's why it's strapped the way it is. Plus, they'll be icing it off and on to keep down the swelling and help with pain."

"Anything that helps," he agreed. He was well aware how intense pain from injuries and surgery could be.

He lowered himself into the chair, stretching out his long legs and adjusting his shoulder. He took a long look at her, studying her face. She had a natural beauty about her that appealed to him the way nothing had for way too long. Telling himself she was injured and recovering from surgery didn't seem to make the feeling go away. It was all he could do to send a silent message to his cock that now, after months of hiding, wasn't the time to wake up and wave.

He sat there for some time watching Lacey, watching the people in the recovery area, studying everyone for signs of a problem. After a while, Natalie came by again to check Lacey's vitals. She had just started the process when a tiny moan drifted from the bed. Wolf looked at Natalie then down at Lacey.

"She's finally coming out of the anesthetic," the nurse said. She touched Lacey's cheek very lightly. "Lacey? Can you open your eyes for me, honey?"

"Mmm." She moved her head slightly and very slowly opened her eyes. "What—How—Where am I?" She slid her glance to Wolf, and her eyes filled with fear.

"It's okay," Natalie told her. "Sheriff Rossi assigned him to you so you'd be protected. It's good he's here. And you can trust him."

Lacey closed her eyes then slowly opened them again, and this time there was a flash of recognition.

"You found me." She swallowed. "You…got me out of the car."

He was stunned she even remembered but pleased she did. It prevented the problem of convincing her to deal with a stranger.

"Along with Sheriff Rossi," he told her, "and two great paramedics."

"My purse. My...camera..."

"I've got them right here." He lifted a bag the hospital had given him to hold everything. "All taken care of."

"Thank...you." She tried to move, pain flashed over her face, and she moaned again.

"Hurts," she murmured.

"I bet it does. You were in a car accident, and you've been shot. You—"

"What? Shot? Who...shot me?" Her face grew even paler if that was possible. "Did you...get him? Did anyone...find Heather?" The fear sharpened. "Oh god. I can't...stay here."

"Listen to me, Lacey." Wolf leaned over her and closed his hand over her free one. "You're safe here, I swear to you. Sheriff Rossi made it very clear what the rules are. That's the first thing for you to know."

"W—What's the second?"

"The second is, we know you're looking for your sister, and the sheriff is on top of it even as we speak. It's an active search. I promise."

She blinked and finally focused her gaze on him. "He—He believes me? Really? I mean, no...one else did. I have to...get out of here. Find my sister."

She lay back on the pillow, obviously exhausted just by that little effort of talking.

"It's being taken care of," Wolf assured her. "Like I said, the sheriff is all over it. So please let the nurse check your vitals and go tell the doctor you're awake so we can get you to a room. The search for your sister is in Alex's capable hands. But there's another problem. Someone is obviously after you, and you need protection. Alex Rossi assigned me to take care of you, and I'm not leaving your side."

Lacey closed her eyes again, but she appeared to relax a little. "I guess that's good. I mean, that finally…someone…takes me seriously."

Wolf wanted to tell her getting shot made everything serious, but he figured he'd wait until she was a little more alert. As he stood beside the bed, waiting for Natalie to get the doctor, another chink in his rusty armor fell by the wayside, and Lacey Cooper became a lot more than a protectee.

CHAPTER 4

HEATHER COLLAPSED on the floor of the rude cabin. She was shaking all over, exhausted by the hours in the dark of evading the two men with guns. She'd only allowed a few moments here and there to rest and gather herself. Over the course of time they'd been doing this, she'd learned how to move almost silently and to avoid the hunters.

She and Trace had figured they'd been here five days. It was hard to tell, since their watches had been taken away.

Trace was already in the cabin when she collapsed into it. He was stretched out on the floor, a nasty scratch on one cheek and another long one on his hand. She took the bandanna that was in her pocket, wet it from one of the very few bottles of water Hunter had left, and began to clean the wounds. She'd been stunned the first time he brought them some, but then Trace pointed out he didn't want them to die of dehydration. He wanted the pleasure of killing them himself. Same with the food they brought. They wanted prey they could hunt, not prey that fell dead at their feet.

"He'll be here soon," she reminded him. "With what passes for our breakfast."

"He's going to be pissed off that we're still alive." Trace dropped his forearm over his eyes.

"I know." Heather dropped down beside him and rested her head on his chest, blinking back unwanted tears. "Trace, I don't know how much longer I can keep this up. I'm so tired."

"We'll make it, babe."

"You say that every day, and I'm trying to believe you. But last night, two of the shots came so close to where I was hiding at the time."

"I have some thoughts about this," he told her. "I've been scoping out all the areas they chase us into, and I think I have an idea. I'm going to check it out tonight."

"If they don't kill us first."

"They won't." His voice was firm. "I have to believe that."

"Besides," she reminded him, "I know Lacey is out there looking for us."

Trace choked out a little laugh. "I bet you're right. When she went two days without hearing from us, she probably flew out here and started yelling at people."

"And thank god for that."

They both knew what a fanatic Lacey was when she focused on something. And family was a number one priority for her.

Heather pulled off her ponytail holder, ran her fingers through her hair, and then pulled it into a tail again. She didn't know why she even cared how she looked. They were filthy and banged up, and their clothes were too bad even for a rag bag. But she had to do little things that were at least some signs they were still human. Some indications they'd escape this.

Come on, Lacey. Do your thing.

She was still kneeling on the dirty floor beside Trace when the door was flung open. Hunter stood there holding two boxes.

"What's this? Getting a little worn down, are we? A little beat up?" His laugh was pure evil. "Don't worry. From the looks of you, this won't last much longer. Although, I do have to say you've been more difficult to hunt than any of our other prey."

"Then maybe you should reward us and let us go," Heather told him.

He clenched his fists and, for a moment, she thought he was going to hit her. Then she watched as he forcibly relaxed them.

"Let you go?" He snorted. "You really think that?"

"You haven't been able to kill us yet," she pointed out, wondering if he was listening to her or ready to hit her. "If that's what the thrill is for you, maybe you need to hunt someone else."

And maybe if we can get out of here, we can prevent that.

He laughed, an evil sound. "The thrill, you say? Interesting. Okay, I will make you a deal, since you're right. The two of you have been very clever quarry. Evade us for two more nights, and we might do just that." Again, that horrible laugh.

"Do you think you're up to it?"

A tiny flame of hope flickered in her chest.

"Do you mean that, or are you just lying to tease us? Play with us."

Oh damn! She wanted to bite her tongue off. She shouldn't have said that. It sounded weak and pleading, and she and Trace had decided to avoid showing weakness as best they could.

"I am a man of my word," he assured her.

Still, Heather didn't believe they could trust him. She and Trace had discussed the man's total arrogance and the tinge of bloodlust in his voice whenever he spoke of the hunt. Trace pushed himself to a standing position and reached for her hand.

"You'll forgive us if we have a hard time believing you."

"Well, then. You'll just have to wait and see." He set the two boxes of food on the floor. "Eat up." He started to leave then turned back. "Maybe this will give you a little more incentive to be creative."

Then he was gone, the lock snicking into place.

Trace pulled Heather into his lap and wrapped his arms around her.

"We're gonna beat this, babe. I promise you." He pressed a gentle kiss on her lips. "I know the odds are stacked against us, but last night as I was zigging and zagging around, I came up with a few ideas. Care to hear them?"

She leaned into his chest. "Yes. Anything. Anything at all that will get us out of this hell."

∼

IT TOOK ONLY another hour in recovery for the doctor to be satisfied that Lacey's condition had improved enough she could leave the area. He signed the orders for her to be moved. Originally, she was slated to be moved to a semiprivate room, but Wolf insisted she have a private one and personally guaranteed the extra charges. For one thing, he couldn't adequately protect her if there was another person in the room, especially if that roommate had visitors. For another, he didn't need a stranger asking questions about why Lacey needed a private security guard, since he would be with her twenty-four seven.

The nurse and the orderly moved her into the bed. The nurse checked her IV and put a fresh cold pack against the area of her arm where she'd been wounded and had the surgery.

As soon as she was settled, he called Alex and gave him the room number.

"How's she doing?" the sheriff asked.

"Actually, pretty damn good, all things considered. She's a real trouper. The bullet lodged in the flesh of her upper arm, but the doctor says she should have minimal damage. And, lucky for her, only a mild concussion and an ugly bump on her forehead. She's woken a few times and managed a few sentences each time, so that's good. I'm hoping to get her out of here in no more than two days."

"As long as it's medically safe," Alex agreed.

"But I'll need someplace to take her to from here. Were you able to find out where she was staying?"

"At one of the campgrounds. Her tent and stuff were still there. I collected everything, and we'll keep it safe for her. Hold on a sec." He was back in a moment. "You obviously can't take her to stay in a tent, even if we left it there. And you already told me you'd look for a place after we had our meeting, so that leaves you without a bed right now. And, Wolf, it's vital that you stay with her."

"Yeah." He snorted. "No kidding. But who knew I'd need a place to take a gorgeous, injured woman, right?"

"Yeah. So here's the thing. When Zane and a couple of other deputies needed to find a place, my wife, Micki, found some good rental properties, each with a couple of acres of land. For privacy. Zane and his wife live in one, Jesse and Terry Donovan in another. She's got a hold on one right now in case things worked out here for you. It's not new, but it's in good condition. I—"

"But we haven't even decided if it's going to work

out between you and me. If you want to hire me, I mean."

And what the fuck would he do if this all fell through?

"I'm not worried. I'm already getting a good sense that you'll fit. Plus, this setup is a good place to keep her secure." He chuckled. "I guess it's become a tradition. I'll text you a couple of photos so you know what it looks like. Micki's going to get the place ready for you, stock some groceries, stuff like that."

"Alex, I don't know if—"

"It's not like there are a lot of choices around here. It's a nice house and rent free until you decide about taking the job. Don't ask." He grinned. "Call it a bribe."

"I don't know what to say." Wolf rubbed his jaw. "I guess we don't have a lot of options, but this is very generous of you and your wife."

"You'll be comfortable there," Alex assured him. "I promise. And there's a nice yard for Bailey to play in."

"That's great. Thank you again."

It certainly was a load off his mind. He couldn't believe how everything was coming together. And just after he'd been ready to write off the rest of his life. One of his former teammates had been a big believer in Fate. "Plan carefully then leave it up to Fate," he used to say. Well, Fate had certainly been looking over his shoulder when Zane Halstead had reached out to him. Maybe the rest of his life wouldn't be a washout after all.

"I've been doing some checking since yesterday," Alex went on. "Lacey reached out to everyone she could contact about her missing sister, but I'll tell you, looking for people in the Crazy Mountains is near impossible unless you have a specific location to start from."

"But if people have disappeared before, surely there's a search and rescue team that has some idea where to look."

"They spent a day on it," Alex assured him. "But again, the area to search is so vast and, with no starting point, it was like hunting a needle in a haystack. They stayed at a bunch of different campgrounds, so even that wasn't a help."

"So, nothing?" Wolf frowned.

"No, but that's not the only odd thing. Hold on." There was a short silence then Alex was back. "I did some digging and got the names of people who had disappeared in the past ten years and were never found."

"Never?" Wolf asked.

"Not even a trace. About twenty in all. There could be more we don't even know about, but this is all I could find."

"Shit."

Alex nodded. "No kidding. Now, some of them could be legitimate. In fact, I'm pretty sure they are. People who got lost in places in the Crazies they were told were unsafe and starved to death in caves or got buried in a rockslide. Or fell off a cliff in an isolated area, of which there are way too many. And sometimes they just pretend to get lost so they can disappear from their lives. But, still..."

"There's a pattern in here somewhere," Wolf pointed out. "I feel it."

"Agreed. I put one of my deputies on it, and he's digging into the background of every name we have. I want to see if there are similarities, either in their histories or in their stay in the area. Something must link them together."

"Good. Keep me in the loop because something doesn't smell right. If Lacey's sister and her fiancé just got swallowed up by the Crazies, why would someone shoot at her?"

"Exactly. Uh, I wanted to check in about Bailey, but I didn't want Kujo to think I didn't trust him."

Alex chuckled. "No sweat. I figured, so I spoke with him. I guess you never know how these things are going to work out, but apparently Six and Bailey have taken to each other like litter mates. He says the biggest problem will probably be trying to figure out how to sleep with both of them in the bed."

Wolf felt himself relax a little.

"Thanks. I really appreciate it."

"He's planning to give you a ring in the morning. See what your schedule is and find out if you guys could work out a few minutes to get together. But, if they discharge Lacey, we can adjust."

"My truck is still at the garage where it was towed, right?"

"Actually, it's at my office. I'll pick you both up if she's discharged and get you to the place where you're staying. We'll have your truck there waiting for you. Also, I got you a temporary carry permit, so that gun you slid into the small of your back is legal."

That was good because the weapon always made him feel more secure. Not that he expected he'd have to shoot it in the hospital, but you never knew. Life was full of many surprises.

"Alex." Wolf searched for the right words. "I don't even know how to thank you."

"Keep Lacey safe. That's thanks enough."

Even though Lacey was asleep, Wolf had gone out into the hallway to take the call, not wanting her to overhear any of it. He was glad he had because when he walked back into the room, she was awake and shifting restlessly in the bed.

"Want your head up a little?" he asked. "The doctor said it would be good for you."

"Please." She studied him through squinted eyes as he raised the bed. "I guess I should be afraid of a strange man in my room, but somehow you don't frighten me."

"Good. That's good." He didn't know if he was presuming too much, but he took the hand of the arm that wasn't in a sling and gave it a gentle squeeze.

"Wait. These meds make me loopy." She frowned. "You were here before." She frowned. "The sheriff brought you. Right?"

"Yes. You were still in recovery, but you were pretty out of it." He grinned. "Like I said, you were pretty out of it, so I'm not surprised you don't remember."

"W-What's your name?"

"Wolf. Wolf Makalski."

"Wolf? That's a weird name. Oh!" She placed her free hand over her mouth. "Sorry. I seem to have lost my manners and the ability to control my mouth."

"No problem. I get that a lot. It means brown. When I was with the Teams, our leader said I always looked like I was hunting like a wolf, and it stuck as my code name. They were a little strange anyway."

She squinted at him. "You, um, kind of look like a wolf."

He wasn't sure if he should be flattered or insulted. "Thanks. I think."

"There was…there was another man. I sort of remember him."

Wolf nodded. "Zane Halstead. One of Sheriff Rossi's deputies. He followed the ambulance here. The sheriff didn't want to leave you unprotected, so Zane had eyes on you from the moment they loaded you onto the stretcher."

"Good. I'm glad I'm not having hallucinations." She moved her left arm, and pain skittered across her face. Her eyes widened, as if she'd just remembered something. "I was shot. In my arm. Right?"

"That's correct."

"Did you... Does anyone... What..." She stopped, her frustration obvious. "God. I can't even talk right."

"Okay, here's what happened. I was driving to a meeting with the sheriff when I found your car crashed into a tree. I called the sheriff who called paramedics, and here you are."

"Just like that?"

He nodded. "Just like that."

"Do you... Does..." She stopped, drew in a shaky breath, and let it out slowly. "Okay. Does anyone know who did it? Who shot me?"

"Not yet." His mouth curved in what he hoped was a reassuring smile. "But if anyone can find them, it's Sheriff Rossi. And his deputies."

"God, I hope so. I've..." She closed her eyes and just lay there breathing slowly.

She closed her eyes and, for a moment, he thought she'd drifted off to sleep again.

"Who are you? Why are you here? I mean, in this room with me?"

"We don't know yet who shot you, and the sheriff is worried whoever it was might come after you again. We want to avoid that." He grinned. "I'm sure you do, too."

"Oh." She was silent for another long moment, as if trying to figure out what to say next. "But you didn't answer the question. Why exactly are you here? In this room with me?" Panic suddenly bloomed in her eyes. "Am I in danger?"

"I won't lie to you. You could be. Someone obviously wants you out of the way, or you wouldn't have ended up with a bullet in your arm. And it could have to do with whatever's happened to your sister and brother-in-law."

He had to battle a strong urge to wrap his arms around her and tell her everything would be okay, even though he knew they were a long way from that. What the fuck was going on with him anyway? He enjoyed women, or at least he had until all the shit happened. But it was always a transient enjoyment, and while he'd had a lot of laughs with them, the main focus was always physical. There might be a strong physical pull between himself and Lacey, but he knew in his gut it was a lot more complex than that. So, what the fuck did he do about it?

He briefly thought about telling Alex he couldn't do this and to assign someone else, but sure as shit, that would be the end of any position here as a deputy. And just when he was shocked to realize his life might be taking an upward turn. No, he'd just have to stick to it. Not hard to do, but he'd have to be sure and keep his dick in his pants and at rest.

"Is something wrong?" Her soft voice broke into his meandering thoughts.

"Only if we don't catch the bad guys." He took her free hand and gave it a gentle squeeze. "But I promise you, that's going to happen. SEALs always catch the bad guys."

She stared at him. "You're a SEAL?"

"Former. Alex, too. And most of his deputies. Why?"

She managed a hint of a smile. "One of my good friends is married to a SEAL. I guess I couldn't ask for a better protector."

Something inside him softened and melted. He was going to be in big trouble here if he didn't watch himself. *Focus, he told himself. Focus on the job.*

"In the interest of full disclosure, I should tell you I left the SEALs more than six months ago on a medical discharge. Our last mission wrecked my shoulder and part of my arm."

"Which one?"

"Left one." He grinned. "We're twins."

She wrinkled her forehead. "If it was hurt that badly, then can you still—"

He held up a hand. "I can still shoot and land a punch if I need to. No worries there. I've been working on it." *Lately, so not really a lie.*

"Oh. Okay. Good." She swallowed with an effort. "Do you think… Is there some water I can have?"

"Oh, sure." *Dummy. He should have thought of that.*

He lifted the cup on her bedside table, filled it from the pitcher, and put a straw in it. Then he raised the head of her bed a little more then held the cup while she drank, slowly.

"Thank you." She wet her lips. "I'm so tired, but who will look for Heather and Trace if I'm in here?"

"I promise you Sheriff Rossi is all over this," he assured her, "and has a couple of his deputies working on it, too. Plus, he's reaching out to others."

"No one I spoke to seemed very optimistic."

She rubbed her forehead with her free hand, wincing slightly as the movement tugged on all her muscles.

"Can you please tell him that I met a man named Cordell Ritchie at a gas station. He said he had something to do with the ranchers, and he'd like to help."

"Sure. I'll pass it along. But now you just need to rest and heal."

"One more thing. When can I get out of here?"

He had to smile. "You're barely out of surgery and still half loopy, plus, I can see it hurts every time you move. Let's see what tomorrow brings."

She shifted slightly and groaned then shook her head.

"I—I guess you're right." She tried to shift again, eliciting another moan, then frowned. "Wait. They won't let me go back to the campground like this, will they? Damn. I have no place else to go, except maybe a motel."

"Right," he agreed, "and not just because of your wound. It's not safe for you there or at a motel where whoever this is can have easy access to you. But the sheriff is working on that, too."

"You mean he's going to put me up someplace? But where? How much will it cost? Besides, I can't stop looking—"

Wolf touched the tip of a finger to her lips.

"Listen, Lacey. Alex has it taken care of and it won't cost you a bundle. Trust me on that. You need to worry less so you'll heal faster. You're lucky there was little muscle damage. And he's looking into your sister's disappearance. I told you that."

"Thank the lord." Lacey closed her eyes and let out a sigh. "He's the first one who is actually doing something, except for the one effort by search and rescue. Everyone told me people disappear in the Crazies, and it's almost impossible to find them."

"Stop worrying about that now."

He reached out for her then shoved his hand in his pockets. Touching her was a big mistake, although he really, unexpectedly, had an intense desire to do so. What the hell was up with him anyway?

"Alex Rossi is an all right guy," he continued. "He has your best interests, as well as your safety, at the top of his list. And again, he's actively on the search. You should just try and get some more rest. You'll heal faster."

"Okay." It came out as a whisper, although with a little reluctance.

"Do you need pain meds?"

She managed a slight shake of her head. "No. They gave me a good shot before we left recovery, and I'm not due for another for a while yet. I'm okay. I'm sure sleep will help."

As he lowered the head of the bed again, just a little, she closed her eyes and, in seconds, was asleep.

He figured while Lacey was knocked out from drugs was a good time to do his daily exercises. Gritting his teeth, he went through the routine, hoping to hell it was working and his shoulder would show at least marginal improvement. He knew he'd never be close to his former physical shape, but if he could just keep his shoulder somewhat limber and his shooting hand in shape, he'd figure out how to be happy with that. After all, he was unexpectedly entering a new chapter of his life and a new career, with people who understood his situation. He was fucking damn lucky, and he'd better appreciate it.

Finished with his routine, Wolf returned to the comfortable recliner some good soul had found for him and adjusted it just enough to stretch out his legs. He couldn't help watching Lacey. The nurse had brushed the snarls out of her hair and washed what little makeup she wore from her face. According to her driver's license, she was thirty-five but, at the moment, she looked ten years younger. He wanted to run his tongue over those full lips and stroke the soft skin of her cheeks. The mounds of her breasts beneath the ugly hospital gown were so tempting. If only—

Jesus Christ, Makalski. Are you some kind of lech? Cut it out!

He was doing his best to think of ice water when his phone vibrated. He pulled it out and looked at the screen. Zane Halstead. As before, he moved out into the hall, pulling the door partially closed behind him but standing directly in front of it to discourage anyone from entering.

"What's up?" he asked.

"How's she doing?" Zane wanted to know.

"Pretty good, all things considered. What's going on?"

"I told Alex I'd give you a call and fill you in on what's happening because he's hot on the scent of this disappearance."

"People keep saying it's impossible to find anyone who disappears in the Crazies," Wolf pointed out. "Has he got something?"

"In some situations, it might not be possible, but I don't think that's going to apply here. Alex had a hunch, so we did a ten-year search for disappearances in the area and found at least eight worth looking into. Certainly with more attention than they got at the time."

"And?"

"There are some similarities that are so strong, the sheriff pulled up everything he could find on the others. Luckily, business is a little slow for us right now, so he's got a couple of us working on it. Recreating things, so to speak."

"You mean, he sees a pattern?" Wolf didn't like the direction this was heading.

"Yes, he does. But where it came from is the big question. He asked Hank Patterson to dial in on this. Hank grew up around here, and if anyone knows what's going on, it would be him. The sheriff is hoping if he points out the similarities, Hank will have some ideas about where others have disappeared and why."

"Hank is the Brotherhood Protectors guy, right?"

"Yes. He's local, so he'd know stuff." Zane laughed. "And he had to promise Alex he wouldn't poach you."

Wolf's eyebrows dove skyward. "Poach me?"

"Uh-huh. Sometimes when Alex brings former SEALs out here hoping to add them as deputies, Hank makes a run at them for Brotherhood Protectors. But I told him if you take any job, it's with us." He paused. "Right?"

Wolf didn't even have to think twice about it. "Yes. Absolutely."

He'd made an instant connection with both Alex and Zane, and he wasn't looking to hook up with anyone else. Not to mention the one between Bailey and Six.

"Before I forget, Lacey wanted me to tell you that someone named Cordell Ritchie approached her at a gas station and said he could organize the ranchers to help.

"Interesting." Zane frowned. "From what we could find out, no one paid more than lip service before this. It's true that disappearances in the Crazies are not uncommon, and only a small percentage of the people are ever found. But Ritchie walks up to a woman he's never met and offers to help? That sends a shiver down my spine. How did he even know what she looks like or who she was?

Wonder where this magnanimous gesture is coming from? I'll tell Alex to check it out."

"Good." He'd learned in the SEALs you never knew where a tiny hint would come from. Or lead to.

"He also wanted me to tell you that Micki—that's his wife—is stocking the house he told you about with groceries. If there's anything you want that's not there—"

"We'll be fine," he interrupted. "I really don't know how to thank everyone."

"Alex will check with the hospital in the morning to see when Lacey is being discharged. If it's tomorrow, he'll pick you up and make arrangements for your truck. Oh, and Bailey, of course."

Wolf didn't know what to say. To be accepted this easily and this quickly was way beyond what he'd expected. He was going to do his damnedest to earn the respect he was being given.

"Okay, will do. And, Zane?"

"Yeah?"

"Thanks. For reaching out to me."

"You're welcome. Listen, being medicalled out of the SEALs is tough on all of us. The period of adjustment can be crushing without at least some kind of help. You'd be surprised how many of us go through it. But we always check out the ones we reach out to very carefully. Alex has made it his mission to reconstitute his staff with former SEALs, especially those who need a new purpose in life. So far, it's working really well."

Wolf raised an eyebrow. "You, too?"

Zane snorted a laugh. "Oh yeah. My situation and how I got here would make a good movie. Sometime I'll tell you about it. Anyway, glad to have you here."

When Wolf walked back into the room, Lacey was moving restlessly in the bed. He was glad the arm they'd operated on was enclosed in a sling to restrict movement. He sure didn't want her tearing out stitches or anything.

He stood beside the bed for a long moment, watching her. He wanted to reach out and stroke her cheeks, try to calm her, silently assure her she was safe, but he was sure if someone walked in, they'd think he was some kind of predator. He wanted her awake and healing so he could see if she felt the same connection he did.

He was still struggling with her effect on him and his reaction to her. He felt as if his life was turning upside down. Which wasn't necessarily a bad thing. But for sure, he'd keep her safe from harm and make sure she got to heal away from danger.

He arranged himself in the chair again. Then he set his phone to vibrate every thirty minutes and placed it in the pocket where he'd be sure to feel it. He'd be fine. He had many years' experience of sleeping in snatches and being able to function.

He closed his eyes and ordered his body to relax. In moments, he was dreaming about an angel with auburn curls dancing naked in front of him.

CHAPTER 5

Lacey struggled to open her eyes, vaguely aware of the pain in her arm and something restricting its movement. She also had a dull headache. When she managed to shift her gaze, the first thing she spotted was the television on a metal arm against a horrible pale-green wall. What? This didn't look like her tent.

She looked around as much as she could and realized she was in a hospital room. Hospital room?

Her eyes landed on the recliner chair on her left and the tall man occupying it. At the moment, his eyes were closed, a ball cap tilted over his face to block the sun streaming in through the window. The edges of dark-brown hair peeked out from beneath the cap. And an equally dark scruff outlined a strong chin and high cheekbones. Long legs were encased in jeans, and a shirt was worn open to expose the T-shirt beneath it. Even in her pain, he was a mouthwatering eyeful.

Oh, great, Lacey. This has to be the most inappropriate time to have sexy thoughts about a stranger.

She shifted slightly and realized the restraint on her arm was a sling. And the arm hurt like hell. A needle was taped into her opposite hand with tubing that led up to a plastic bag filled with…something. And she realized instead of her shirt and jeans, she was wearing some kind of hospital clothing.

What on earth?

Then it all came slamming back to her. The shot, the bullet smashing the window and hitting her arm, the crash into the tree and then…nothing. Oh, wait! She woke up a few times and actually talked to someone. A man. Was it the one in the chair? She struggled to remember who he was and what he'd told her. She tried to reach for the button to call the nurse and groaned as pain burned her upper left arm.

The man in the chair was instantly awake and beside her so fast, she wondered if she'd imagined him sleeping.

"Hold on."

His voice was deep with a slightly rough edge. But instead of frightening her, that sound wrapped itself around her like a warm blanket. Now she remembered. Wolf Makalski. Holy shit! She was in a hospital room with a man she'd never met until last night, and she was attracted to his voice? What kind of drugs were they giving her anyway?

He rested his fingertips on her shoulder for a

moment, as if to calm her then found the call button and pressed it.

She squinted up at him, still trying to focus her eyes. Holy mother! Even in her damaged state, she couldn't miss how sexy he was. A very masculine face with a square jaw highlighted by a neatly trimmed scruff beard. Sharp cheekbones were softened by incredibly long eyelashes and a sensuous mouth. Brown hair clipped close to the head.

And what was the matter with her that now of all times she was noticing these things?

But she also noted the hard look in his eyes, as if he'd seen too many nightmares or maybe lived through them. What was his story?

That damn curiosity of hers was working overtime, even in circumstances like this.

None of my business. But still...

"The nurse should be here in a second," he told her. "Would you like some water?"

She ran her tongue over her parched lips. "Yes, please."

She also had to go to the bathroom but she needed help from the nurse. What the hell was she going to do when they let her out of here? Meanwhile, she took slow sips of water through the straw.

"Wolf." She looked up at him. "Right?"

"Yes. Glad you remembered."

"You were nice to me." She closed her eyes. "Sorry. That was a stupid thing to say. This stuff they gave me plus what I'm sure is left of the anesthetic really scrambles my brain."

"Been there, done that." He shrugged. "And maybe a lot of people haven't been nice to you lately."

"They've been politely rude," she told him, "if you can understand that."

"Oh, yeah. Definitely had it happen to me."

"Are you going with me to...wherever I'm going from here? I have no idea where my car is." She made a face. "Not that I could drive. But I don't know what's happening. With anything."

"Your car is at the garage being fixed. They hauled it out of the ditch where you landed. And I have a place to take you, a house, where we'll be the only ones there, out of traffic. Out of visibility. Just in case. Sheriff Rossi made the arrangements."

"Just in case? You think whoever this is would try again? In the hospital?"

Wolf shrugged. "Anything is possible and, from what I gather, Alex isn't a guy to take chances. If it's someone you know he—or she—could easily waltz in here."

Lacey wasn't afraid of much but this scared the hell out of her. Someone she knew? How was that possible? She'd only been in Montana a couple of weeks. Something clicked in her scrambled brain.

"You're the one who found me, aren't you? I don't know how I know that, but I do."

He nodded. "Yes. I did. And before you ask again,

Alex is all over the situation with your sister and her fiancé. If anyone can find them, it's him." His mouth tilted in a tiny grin. "He's a former SEAL after all."

Before she could ask him anything else the nurse hurried in.

"Oh, Miss Cooper. Glad to see you're awake. Good, good. How's the arm?"

Lacey probed it gently with the fingertips on her free hand. "Hurts like a bitch, but I'll live. And the bump on my head doesn't hurt so much."

"It looks like your IV is finished. Let's get that needle out of your arm so you can at least have one free hand to move. I brought a pain pill for you, which you should take right now since you'll be moving around and that wound is still fresh. They'll give you a prescription for pain when you're discharged, plus antibiotics which you'll need to take for ten days. Let me just check your vitals, and we'll get you cleaned up." She looked at Wolf. "Outside, please. I'll let you know when we're done."

Wolf nodded. "Yes, ma'am."

As soon as he was out of the room, the nurse began tending to Lacey.

"Your top and jeans are pretty much a mess, being covered in blood. We put them in your locker. I've got a fresh set of scrubs for you. I made sure the top was a couple of sizes too big so it would be easier to put on and take off."

"I have clothes," she told the nurse. "They're—"

She stopped. Where were they, exactly? The last she knew, they'd been stashed in her trunk. She didn't like to leave them when she left her tent for the day. Oh god! Had someone just taken everything?

"I'm sure that hunk that's with you took care of it," the nurse assured her. "We'll leave the sling off for now, unless the doctor wants you to put it back on. Lucky for you, there are no bullet fragments, but I'd restrict the use of that arm for a few days."

Lacey managed a little laugh. "Don't worry. That won't be a problem."

"Oh, and the gentleman has your purse."

Her purse! She stupidly hadn't even given it a thought. She'd get it from Wolf when he came back into the room.

By the time she finished in the bathroom and got cleaned up, she was exhausted and her arm hurt like a son of a bitch. She was happy to lie down on the bed again. The nurse opened the door and motioned Wolf into the room.

"How about some breakfast?" she asked Lacey. "I'm guessing it's been a while since you last ate."

The thought of food made her nauseous. "Maybe just some tea?"

"Okay, if you're sure. But you should think about eating something before too long." She glanced over at Wolf. "Coffee or tea for you, too?"

"No, that's okay. Thanks. I'm good."

"If you say so. The doctor will be by in a bit," she

told him. "If you'll be the one taking care of her, he'll give you instructions. That arm needs to be checked regularly for swelling. If there is any, ice is the best remedy. And we also want to make sure there's no infection."

"Got it covered," Wolf assured.

He did? Would he be changing her dressing and giving her the medication? She hardly knew him, yet…yet…there was a feeling that with this man she'd be safe no matter what. Does the sheriff know I was shot?" she asked him then shook her head. "Of course he does. That's how I got here. Does he have any idea who did it? And why? And does it have something to do with Heather and Trace?"

"Yes, but he doesn't have specific answers to either question yet. He thinks, though, it might have something to do with your sister's disappearance."

"Really? He actually took me seriously?" She stared up at him.

"Oh, he took you very seriously," he assured her.

"I've been trying for two weeks to get someone to do more than pay lip service to it. Are you telling me he thinks it's more than them just getting lost?" She couldn't believe he wasn't brushing her off with platitudes like almost everyone else had done.

Wolf nodded. "He does. And even though he and I just met, so I don't yet know him well, I'd bet everything on him finding the answer. SEALs never give up."

"I've heard." She had to smile. "I'm guessing you were a SEAL, too."

He nodded, and, for a moment, a look somewhere between bitterness and anger flashed across his face. Then the faint smile returned.

"You don't mind going to this house with me, wherever it is? Being my babysitter?"

"He'll be more than a babysitter," a deep male voice answered. "I needed someone trained in protection and dealing with enemies until we find your sister and her fiancé and catch whoever is behind this."

Lacey looked at the man in a sheriff's uniform who walked in. It could have been any deputy, but she was sure this was Alex Rossi himself. Wolf confirmed it when he greeted him.

"Morning, Sheriff. Checking on our patient?"

"Absolutely. Lacey, I'm Alex Rossi. How are you doing this morning?"

"Um, not too bad." She managed a smile. "Thank you for coming by. I didn't expect to have our meeting in a hospital."

"Neither did I. How are you feeling?"

She wanted to tell him her arm felt like someone stuck an arrow into it and left it there, but she hated complaining. Besides, she was pretty sure a former SEAL and current sheriff had experienced much more serious wounds. Instead, she somehow managed a smile.

"Everyone keeps asking. My arm hurts, and my head aches, but I'm alive so that's good, right?"

"It is for sure. Listen, I called the hospital director this morning. He said they'll be releasing you as soon as the doctor has checked you one more time. You—"

"To the house Wolf told me about? Is it expensive? I have credit cards—"

She forced herself to draw a breath. The pain in her arm had abated somewhat, as long as she didn't move it around much. The pain pill was doing its job and the nurse had told her they'd give her a prescription when she was discharged. For the moment, she could somewhat unscramble her brains.

Alex Rossi exchanged a look with Wolf.

"Yes, we've got you set up in a nice place. Nothing fancy, but you'll be comfortable. There's no charge. It's part of my wife's contribution to my SEAL recruitment and, before you say anything, she can afford it." He grinned. "I married an heiress."

"Oh."

Then his face sobered and, for a moment, a bitter look flashed in his eyes. But it was gone so fast, she wondered if she'd imagined it. He looked at Wolf again then back at her.

"You've obviously poked someone hard enough with your questions that they wanted to scare you off. And until we find out what happened with your sister and her fiancé, you'll have full-time protection. Wolf will be staying there with you."

"He told me."

If she wasn't so emotionally on edge because of Heather and Trace, and riding the edge of pain because of her arm and her head, she might have actually been a little excited. Who wouldn't want to be locked away with a very sexy former SEAL?

Plus, it would be stupid to object. She had no other lodging, and she certainly couldn't protect herself. But locked away with Wolf Makalski? It unsettled her that in her current physical state, plus the crisis with Heather and Trace, she could be wildly attracted to this man she'd just met. How improper was that?

"I had your car towed," Alex continued. "The front end was smashed pretty good, but the garage we use will do a good job fixing it. I'll text you a copy of the accident report for your insurance company."

"Thank you." Something else to hassle with. How much worse could things get? Oh, wait. They might never find Heather and Trace. That would be much worse.

"I've also got all your stuff from the campground. I locked everything but your clothes in my office. The clothes I took to the house where you'll be staying, and my wife put them away."

She was stunned. "I—I don't know what to say."

"You don't need to say anything. The doctor should be by to see you pretty soon," he went on. "I'm going to drive the two of you to the house you'll be using. Kujo is meeting us there with your truck, Alex, and with Bailey."

"Bailey?" Lacey looked from one to the other. "Who's Bailey."

Wolf sighed. "Bailey's my dog. A beautiful Belgian Malinois. He got his medical discharge when I did." He paused and looked at her. "You're not afraid of dogs, are you? Or allergic to them?"

She stared from one man to the other then just shrugged.

"No, I love dogs." What else could she say. "I feel like I'm living someone else's life. And what about Heather and Trace? Have you found any indications at all about what might have happened to them?"

"Not yet, but I've only been on it since yesterday. Believe me. We'll talk about it when we get to the house. I want to know every single thing you can tell me."

"I'll tell you whatever I know. Everything I found out. It isn't much though."

"Whatever you can tell me will help."

And Wolf would be there. With her. How is it possible she felt a connection with this man she hadn't even known twenty-four hours ago? Was it the danger of the situation? The—The what? She hoped her instincts where Wolf was concerned weren't malfunctioning because she felt safe with him, and she knew safety was something she was going to need in large doses.

Before anyone could say anything else, the doctor

walked in to check Lacey's arm and her head. And then she was getting her discharge papers, she was being wheeled out to the patient exit, and Wolf was helping her into his fancy truck. She had a deep-down feeling her life was about to change drastically in many, many ways.

CHAPTER 6

Hunter was doing his best to keep his temper under control. If there was one thing he hated it was busybodies, and Lacey Cooper topped the list. For two years, since they'd started playing The Hunt, he and his game partner had created a situation where people disappearing in the Crazy Mountains were just written off as swallowed up in that environment. Oh, there had been some search and rescue canvasses, but predictably they had turned up nothing. As long as Hunter could remember—and that was a good long time—unless there was a definite starting point, people just disappeared and were never found.

Of course, Hunter knew where they were: buried in the farthest corner of his property in unused, forested acreage where they'd never be found. He'd planned this very well, right from the beginning. The satisfaction of finally killing the prey was unlike anything he'd ever felt before. Humans were a much more satisfying hunt than animals. And, as a bonus, it aroused him so much, he'd drive into Livingston or even Billings, pick up a willing female, and fuck her until his dick finally signaled it had had enough.

But these human targets were becoming a problem. It would spoil the game to just shoot them out of frustration, but he was about ready to put an end to it all. Things looked like they might be getting complicated. He needed to do it before Lacey, that bitch of a sister, drummed up too much interest. He'd carefully created a situation that he thought would discourage her, but no. She was still fucking around.

He'd taken a big chance shooting at her. He'd had to do some quiet investigating to see where she would be and when she'd be there. Then he had to figure out the best place to take his shot and make a quick exit. His plan was to put her out of commission before she got someone to take her seriously. By then, this hunt would be over, the prey disposed of, and he could retire from the game for a while.

He had managed to find a way to quietly insinuate himself into the situation, working with search and rescue when they did their one pass at it and mentioning it to people who needed to know. He figured if another search was mounted, he could steer it in the wrong direction.

But then he learned by listening to local gossip that the sheriff, Alex Rossi, had brought in another damn former SEAL to hire as a deputy and assigned him to guard Lacey. That presented two problems. One, fucking SEALs never let go of anything. Two, with this guy plus Alex digging into this, he could be in big trouble.

He had to find out where Lacey Cooper would be staying and figure out how to arrange an accident for her that didn't present questions. Otherwise, this persistent nosy bitch was going to destroy what he and his co-hunter had built up for the past ten years.

Damn it all to fucking hell anyway.

But getting that information wouldn't be easy. Utilizing it would be even harder.

Think, he told himself. How could he accomplish this in a casual and acceptable way that did not raise a red flag? Because he was sure the fucking sheriff had radar that could pick up even the most obscure signals.

He finished his coffee, standing by the kitchen window, looking at the scene outside. Ten thousand acres rolled away from the massive house, acres stocked with prime Angus cattle. He was the third generation to own this ranch, growing it even bigger than it was before. He'd followed the pattern by becoming active in the ranchers association and community activities.

When he married, it was only to create children so he'd have someone to hand the ranch over to. He chosen a woman who was already part of the ranching community and whose physical attributes would produce good-looking children. Quiet. Polite. Portraying just the image he needed. Well, the joke was on him. Claire had turned out to be a bitch of the first order, ice-cold in bed once the ring was on her finger and, the worst blow of all, unable to conceive children. But divorcing her would have been expensive. Besides, she gave him the appearance of respectability, a good cover for his very private activities.

He'd been wrestling with that problem and looking for something new to focus on when the idea of The Hunt was conceived. The emotional high he got from it was almost as good as an orgasm. Almost. He'd discovered there was no shortage of prey. And every hunt had been successful. Until now. Pure bad luck was threatening to derail the game. He and his partner could not let that happen. If he wanted to continue the game, he had to eliminate Lacey Cooper.

He sighed. This would take a lot of time and concentration. Maybe he should put a pause in The Hunt for tonight. It would give that couple—his current prey— a false sense of security and make the final days that much more exciting.

The best place to pick up information without raising eyebrows was The Horseshoe in Eagle Rock. He'd already had breakfast, but he could always use another one, along with the restaurant's incredible muffins. He patted his flat abdomen. He could afford a few calories. And people seemed to talk more freely when you were chewing food. There was a reason the place was called Gossip Central.

Then the tricky part would be getting close enough to her without being caught out. But he could figure out a way to do that. Right?

He rinsed his mug, left it in the sink, and headed out to his truck. Time to do a little digging that had nothing to do with soil.

∼

Lacey sat tensely in her seat as Alex drove down the gravel driveway. They had passed some houses on the main road, but they were all pretty well spaced apart. Lots of land with them. Was the place where she'd be staying like that? She had no idea what to expect of it or how things would play out between her and Wolf. He had been super attentive in the hospital, but that had all taken place in less than twenty-four hours. Would that continue? Would he now feel she was an unwanted obligation? Something he hadn't bargained for?

And what did she do about this very unexpected attraction to him? Her arm hurt, her head ached, yet at the same time, her body throbbed with unexpected desire. She was just an unholy mess.

Her eyes widened as they reached the end of the driveway. The house was built to look like a log cabin, with a gabled roof and two steps leading up to a porch. To the right was a garage with a couple of trucks parked in front of it. To the left of that was a small barn. Behind the barn, she saw an empty corral, and beyond that a nice expanse of green, dotted with Ponderosa pine. If she hadn't been in pain and on edge, she might have appreciated the landscape and situation.

Wolf climbed out of the truck and opened the passenger door for Lacey. They had fixed her up in the shotgun seat, propping pillows around her injured arm to make her as comfortable as possible on the drive. She had to smile at the way he was obviously trying to figure out the best way to help her take the big step out.

"What the hell," he muttered under his breath. He picked her up in his arms and lifted her from the vehicle. When he gritted his teeth, she frowned.

"Are you hurt?"

"Just the damn leftover from my last mission as a SEAL. It's fine. Ignore it. I'm more concerned about your injury than mine."

When he set her on her feet, he was careful not to jostle her arm, but as her body slid down his, for a moment, as their eyes connected, she was shocked to feel heat flash through her. Was that an answering flare she saw for just a moment in his eyes? Then it was gone, and he just made sure she was steady on her feet.

"Ready to look inside?" Alex asked.

"Okay."

Wolf placed his hand on Lacey's uninjured elbow,

guided her inside, and helped her to a chair in the living room.

"Nice." He looked around the room warmed by the sun coming in through the large windows. Then he turned to Alex. "I'm sure I don't know how to thank you."

Alex chuckled. "I'm sure we'll find a way."

At that moment Kujo came out of the kitchen, a struggling Bailey on the end of a leash. Lacey stared at the gorgeous animal, strangely unafraid of him. She could see he was quivering all over as he stared at Wolf with anticipation.

"I had to leash him up," Kujo laughed, "or he'd have run outside before you all even got out of the truck."

He snapped off the leash, and the dog hurried to Wolf's side. Then he sat and waited impatiently for the command to move.

Wolf nodded and snapped his fingers.

"*Vrij.*" Go ahead.

The dog stood and rubbed his head against Wolf's hand then against his thigh then licked his hand. Wolf crouched down and rubbed the dog's head, letting Bailey lick his face.

"Miss me, did you?" he laughed.

"He was very well-behaved," Kujo told him, "and he and Six did really well together, but he definitely wanted you around."

"I thought you might bring Six with you."

"Next time," Kujo promised. "I wanted Bailey to

settle into his new home first. Although they got along like they'd known each other forever while he's been staying with us."

"We've been together a long time." Wolf rose to his feet. "Lacey, meet my better half. Bailey."

She wasn't sure if she should reach for him or what, but Wolf touched his hand to hers then guided it to Bailey's head. She stroked him, and then the dog laid his head on her leg and looked up at her with soulful eyes.

"Oh!" She couldn't help smiling. "He's wonderful." She managed to lean forward and place a kiss on his head.

"Careful," Wolf teased. "I might sue you for alienation of affections."

Kujo cleared his throat. "Okay, I can see things are good around here. Get yourselves settled and Molly and I will bring Six over to visit." He looked at Lacey. "Molly really wants to meet you, if that's okay. She's been in your shoes before."

"She was looking for a relative?" Lacey asked.

"No, she was in a dangerous situation where her life was in jeopardy. In her case, terrorists tried to kill her. I don't think your shooter was a terrorist, but it's definitely someone dangerous."

"Tell her thanks, and I'd love to meet her. I mean, as soon as I get myself together."

"Duly noted." He looked at Wolf. "I picked up some breakfast pastries on the way over. I didn't know if you'd eaten or if Lacey would even be hungry. That should at least tide you over."

"Thanks, man. I'll grab one in a few. Lacey?" He looked over at her. "How about a little something to absorb those meds they gave you?"

She shook her head. "Not now. I don't think I could eat anything."

"You have to get something in your stomach, or you'll be sick. How about just part of a plain pastry?"

"Um, okay. And I'd love some tea, if possible. If it's not a problem, I mean."

"I can take care of that, and it's not a problem." He crouched down so he was at eye level with her. "Nothing is a problem, Lacey. And it's my pleasure to do it. Really."

If he was putting on an act, it was a really good one.

He was about to head toward the kitchen when Alex pulled a chair up close to Lacey's. Wolf's eyes widened when Bailey moved over and plunked himself down next to her, alert, as if at attention. He looked at Alex, and a low growl rumbled in his throat.

Wolf burst out laughing. "I guess I don't have to worry how he'll react around you."

Alex grinned. "And I guess I'd better be on my best behavior."

"Yeah. Keep that in mind."

"If you're up to it," the sheriff said, "I need to get every bit of information from you I can. Details of when you discovered your sister and her fiancé had gone missing, all about your search, anything you did or did not find." He looked at Wolf. "Think she's up to it?"

"*She* can speak for herself," Lacey snarked. "And it doesn't matter how I feel. Finding Trace and Heather tops everything, so fire away."

She shifted in her chair then drew a frown from both men when she bumped her arm and winced.

"Then *she* better be more careful with herself," Wolf told her. "Let me get something for that arm."

He disappeared in the direction of the kitchen. When he returned, he had some ice wrapped in a dish towel which he rested against her arm. That he even thought of that made her heart warm even more. And other parts of her body, which shocked her. She could sense him watching her carefully, ready to put a stop to things if he thought she was too weak or ill. As if drawn by an invisible thread, she looked up at him and gave a tiny nod of her head. He smiled and there went that flash of heat again.

"That would be good. And, Sheriff Rossi—"

"Alex, please."

"Alex. Okay. I don't want to waste any time. I don't know what I can tell you but I'll do anything to find them." She glanced at Wolf. "I have a feeling we've lost time already."

"Got it, but let's take things easy. I'll go take care of the tea and toast."

"Micki will have stocked some," Alex told him. "It's one of her staples."

"Great. Hold on, Lacey, and I'll get it fixed. How about one of those pastries?"

"Not right now. Maybe later." She blew out a breath. "I certainly hate imposing on everyone. Not to mention having a man I just met wait on me."

"You're in no condition yet to be wandering around a strange kitchen," Wolf pointed out. "And I'm happy to do it."

"Then yes, that would be very nice. Thank you."

A funny little feeling wiggled its way through her. She tried to figure out what was causing her reaction to this man. Was it the unusual circumstances, the danger of the situation she found herself in? Was it the huge lapse of time since her last relationship? But that had ended so badly, she'd been sure she never wanted another one. Ever.

Wolf, however, was so different than the other men she'd known. He wasn't full of himself, boasting about how macho he was or strutting for other women, like the nurses in the hospital. Maybe it was because he was the real deal, while the others had been wannabes. Okay, in the midst of a crisis, why was she even thinking that about a man she'd known barely twenty-four hours?

Good lord, Lacey.

And he seemed genuinely concerned about her. She just hoped she wasn't misreading him or that it wasn't all a big act.

"I'll go ahead and get your stuff out of the trucks, Wolf," Kujo said. "Then, if no one minds, I'd like to sit in on the discussion. I figure the more information I can bring back to Brotherhood Protectors, the more we'll be able to help. Hank's pretty pissed off about people disappearing forever in his backyard."

"Yeah, thanks." Alex nodded. "We'll take all the help we can get. In fact, after I talk to Lacey, I'm thinking of calling a community meeting like we've done before, to enlist everyone in the search. You never can tell what someone knows until you jog their memory."

Kujo nodded. "Good idea."

"Have you heard anything yet?" Lacey asked the sheriff. "Anything at all?"

He shook his head. "No, but it's been less than twenty-four hours since I put out the first feelers. I have two of my other deputies asking questions and looking around, plus Kujo will take everything you tell me back to Brotherhood Protectors, and they'll get on it. You can't have better people doing this."

"Thank you." She looked at Kujo. "You, too. After being shut down by just about everyone I'd spoken to and getting absolutely nowhere, I can't believe something is finally happening." Her mouth twisted in a small grimace of pain. "Maybe it was worth getting shot after all."

Wolf returned with a steaming mug of tea and set it on the table next to her chair. He also carried an actual ice wrap in his hand.

"Micki thought of everything," he told her as he removed the towel and fastened the wrap around her upper arm.

"Oh god, that feels so good." She sighed. "Thank you."

"The instructions said twenty minutes at a time, so I'll time it."

Then he pulled an ottoman up to her chair. Bailey padded over to them and rested his chin on Wolf's thigh. He studied Lacey with soulful eyes.

She smiled at him. "Is he guarding me?" she asked.

"He's a natural protector," Wolf told her. "I know he senses you are in danger. That's part of what made him such a valuable member of our team. I think he's connected with you, and that doesn't usually happen so fast."

Lacey smoothed her hand over Bailey's head, and he pressed it against her palm. "Well, I feel honored. Thank you, Bailey."

As she picked up the mug, she gave silent thanks that she'd been shot in her left arm and not her right. At least she wasn't completely helpless. She was also damn glad that Wolf Makalski and Bailey had been the ones to find her.

She took a slow sip of the steaming liquid and nodded in approval. "This is good. Thanks so much, Wolf." She settled more comfortably in the chair. "Okay, Sheriff, I'm ready."

"Alex, please. And if you need a break at any time, just please let me know."

It took the better part of an hour, what with answering all the questions, before both Alex and Wolf were satisfied they had every bit of information she knew. Kujo threw in a few questions of his own. When she finished, though, she was convinced that if anyone could find Heather and Trace, it was these people.

Wolf had never left her side the entire time. He refilled her tea once, asked if she needed anything else, asked twice if she needed a break.

"No." She shook her head. "Thanks for checking, but I just want to get it all out so there can be some action." She looked at Alex. "And you. I have no idea how to thank you."

"It's my job, Lacey, and I'm sorry that so many people around here have let you down. But we'll find them. I promise." He smiled at her. "And SEALs never break a promise."

"If you give me the scripts," Kujo said, "I'll run them in to the pharmacy. Alex, I know you've got stuff to do, so I'll just drop you off first. And, Wolf, you won't be leaving this woman's side even for a second, so I'm happy to do this."

"I put your rifle on the kitchen counter," Alex told him. "I assume you saw it there. I left you a couple boxes of ammo and also for your handgun. I wasn't sure how much you had."

"Appreciate it. I like being prepared, even if I never have to use it."

"Also, I want to give you the laptop the security

system is hooked into. It monitors several locations. It was hard to decide where to put sensors what with wild animals roaming around. However, we've got cameras in all the trees close to the house and in two of the stands of trees farther out. And there are sensors all around the area close to the house, so nobody will be able to sneak up on you without warning."

Wolf nodded. "Good deal."

"Thank you, Sheriff." Lacey was overwhelmed at the lengths that this man had gone to in order to protect her. But it also made her nauseous to think of how bad they must think Heather and Trace's situation was and the dangerous people they must have run into. She was even more astounded that these strangers were willing to jump in and take care of her without hesitation. When this was all over, she'd have to make sure they knew how much she appreciated it.

Alex left with Kujo, who was driving him to his office, and Lacey leaned back in her chair, closing her eyes. She'd done nothing but sit and talk, yet she was exhausted. And her arm was throbbing. She was glad they'd given her a few pain pills at the hospital because she sure could use one now.

As if he'd read her mind, Wolf appeared at her side, a pill in one hand, a glass of water in the other. She swallowed it gratefully.

"It's about lunchtime," he told her. "Would you like something to eat? I mean, if the pastries don't appeal to you, I can actually cook. That is, if it's not complicated."

"Good to know, but I think I'd rather lie down for a little bit first. You should go ahead and eat though."

"I will if I get hungry."

Lacey shook her head. "I can't believe I got so wiped out from doing nothing."

"You've been through a lot in less than twenty-four hours," he reminded her. "Come on. I'll help you get settled in your room."

She saw the house had three nice-size bedrooms, and all the beds had been made up. The largest one, the master suite where Wolf guided her, had its own en-suite bath. She noticed there was even a bouquet of flowers on the dresser. Alex definitely had a gem for a wife.

By the time she got to the bed, the pill was already beginning to take effect. Without making a big deal out of it, Wolf pulled back the covers on the bed and patted the space for her to sit. Then he removed her shoes.

"Are you, uh, going to need help with anything here?" he asked. "You shouldn't sleep in the hospital clothes."

She would have laughed at his discomfort if she weren't so tired.

"I think I can handle it myself. Can you just turn your back for a minute? I promise to call you if I need help."

When he looked away, she managed to wriggle

out of the pants, using only one hand. The top, however, was another matter. Maybe she'd do it later. Exhausted just from that little effort, she sat back down on the bed and pulled the edge of the covers across her lap.

"You can turn around now."

She almost laughed at the look on his face and the way he tried to avert his eyes from her legs sticking out from the edge of the covers.

"Um, you okay here?"

"I don't want to wrestle with the top right now. If you could just help me lie back and fix my pillows for me? And pull the covers up the rest of the way? That would be great."

She swallowed a smile at the look on his face, determination not to look anywhere but at the covers themselves. But what was up with her, wanting to throw them back and have him touch her? Maybe the bump on her head yesterday had disturbed her brain.

But Wolf did it the same way she assumed he'd gone about his tasks as a SEAL—quietly and efficiently. He helped her lie back and lifted her legs until she was lying prone. Then he tucked the covers over her. She had to ignore the sudden heat from that touch alone.

"I'll leave the door open," he told her. "Just holler if you need anything."

"Thank you."

He stood there, looking down at her for a long moment. It shocked her that her whole body reacted to that look. Her nipples hardened, her skin heated and, between her legs, a pulse began to throb most inappropriately. Holy hell! What was going on with her? She'd been shot, and Heather and Trace were missing god knew where, and suddenly she had the hots for a man who was still a stranger?

Get it together, Lacey.

No, not a stranger, she told herself. There was something about this quiet, very masculine man that touched every part of her. She'd known him for less than twenty-four hours, for god's sake, but there was a raw masculinity about him that stirred everything inside her. A hungry need that hadn't been a part of any relationship for a very long time surged through her and nested in every corner of her body. She couldn't stop thinking about what he'd look like naked. She wanted to know how it would feel to press herself against the hard wall of his chest, to feel the hard outline of his cock against her. To feel—

Holy crap. She needed to turn off whatever this was that was taking over her body. She was grateful that luck had brought Wolf into her life, probably saved her from bleeding to death. And now he was going to be her bodyguard twenty-four seven, something she hadn't ever thought she'd need. She'd better be on her best behavior so she didn't embarrass herself. Or worse, send him running for the hills.

She was still running it all through her mind when she dozed off.

They were lying facing each other on the bed, naked

bodies pressed together. Hard pecs pressed against her breasts with their swollen nipples, and his thick cock nudged the mound of her sex. His mouth brushed against hers, the beard tickling her skin. His tongue traced the seam, and she opened her mouth willingly. When his tongue swept inside, she sucked hard on it, the little groan it elicited sending heat flashing through her. This man was pure sex on a stick, so masculine yet with a gentler side. Giving herself to him was easy, especially when he lit a fire inside her that had been dormant for so long.

One large hand slid down her arm and moved to cup a breast, his fingers pinching and teasing the nipple. She moaned at the spear of pleasure and arched herself to his touch.

"I could do this forever," he murmured. "I love the feel of those hard nipples and your gorgeous breasts."

He bent his head to take a nipple into his mouth, sucking on it and letting his teeth graze the pebbled skin before taking a little bite. At once, the pulse in her sex began to throb with insistent need. She threw one leg over his and pressed her mound against him, hungry for the feel of his hot thick shaft against her.

His soft laugh rumbled against her skin.

"A little anxious, are we?"

She wanted to tell him, Yes! Very anxious! But slow was good, too.

As he feasted on first one breast and then the other, she slid one hand between their bodies and wrapped her fingers around his swollen dick. When she ran her thumb over, the soft the feel of a tiny drop of liquid excited her even more. He was hot for her, this very sexy, very masculine man was revved up for her body.

As he worked his way down from her breasts over her stomach, pausing to twirl the tip of his tongue at her navel, the hunger in her ramped up even more. She wanted to shout Yes! When he urged her over onto her back, he nudged her thighs apart, and ran the tips of his fingers down the seam of the lips of her sex.

"Wet," he whispered. "So wet. I love how wet you are for me."

He stroked his fingers up and down between the folds, each time brushing her clit and sending hot streaks of electricity through her. She squeezed her thighs together, trapping his hand and riding it as he moved it faster and faster. When he moved it enough to slip two fingers inside her, she pushed down on them, dug her heels into the bed, and rode them as hard as she could.

The orgasm struck almost without warning, shaking her body, her inner walls spasming around his fingers. Her body shook with the force of it, and she squeezed her thighs together as hard as she could, riding his hand.

At last, the tremors subsided and she lay there, catching her breath, as...

Lacey's eyes popped open and for a moment she was disoriented. Then she realized her free hand, under the covers, was between her thighs and lazily stroking her sex. Her body felt as if she'd just had an orgasm, and crap! When she eased her fingers up and found them sticky, she realized that's exactly what had happened.

She looked around at the strange room, for a moment unsure exactly where she was. She didn't recognize anything, including the furniture. What was she doing in a strange bedroom bringing herself to orgasm and…

Crap!

Wolf's face popped into her brain; the dream came back with her and Wolf naked. As she realized what she'd just done, she wanted to pull the covers over her head and hide forever. She was in this strange house. With Wolf. Having sexually explicit dreams. She moved, pain shot through her arm, and it all came flashing back to her. Heather. Trace. The lack of answers. Getting shot. Meeting Wolf.

Oh, yes. Wolf. The man with whom she'd just had imaginary sex. Except apparently it wasn't all that imaginary. And how had she forgotten, even for a little while, about Heather and Trace? When she glanced at the door and realized it was partially open, the hot flashes she got had nothing to do with sex. Had Wolf peeked in to check on her? Had seen her bringing herself to orgasm? God! What must he think of her?

It had to be the pill she'd taken. What else could bring on such an erotic dream when she was recovering from a fresh bullet wound?

Being careful of her bad arm, she shifted a little, pulled the covers up to her chin with one hand, and closed her eyes. Maybe she could go back to sleep and, when she woke up, it would all have disappeared. But she had barely closed her eyes again when she heard a soft tapping on the partially open door. She tried to ignore it and pretend she was still sleeping, but the tapping sounded again.

"Lacey?" He spoke very softly, just in case she was still asleep.

She heard a little whining sound. Bailey! She hoped Wolf didn't sue her for alienation of affections.

"You awake?" Wolf persisted. "You okay?"

She wanted to say *Do I look like I'm awake*, but she figured she must have been out for a long time for him to disturb her. Still, she lay there with her eyes closed, trying to straighten out her brain before answering. Being hidden away with this very sexy man might not be the best solution here. She was just darn glad he hadn't walked into the room earlier.

"Hey. You okay?"

Okay? She almost giggled at the question, wondering exactly how she should answer him.

CHAPTER 7

Wolf looked at Lacey lying in the bed and waited for her to answer him. Bailey had come to sit beside him and now nudged his leg and whined softly.

"I know, I know. I want her to wake up, too, so we can make sure she's okay. Just give it a minute."

She'd been sleeping for almost three hours and, while he'd checked on her a couple of times already, this last time nearly rocked his socks off. Was it his dirty mind that imagined she'd been bringing herself to orgasm?

He thought about how fast things had accelerated since yesterday when he was driving leisurely along a two-lane highway for a meeting with Alex Rossi. He'd gotten here because he was a former SEAL, and he was staying for the same reason. Because being a SEAL meant a lot more than just excelling in your work. SEALs knew from day one they must earn their Trident every single day. Their uniform was a calling. In his bitterness and misery and self-pity, he had forgotten that.

Zane Halstead reaching out to him might have been the trigger to reverse the process, but finding Lacey Cooper in that car had really pushed his buttons. Now, all his SEAL training was reasserting itself, his instincts at full force. And, for whatever reason, the constant discomfort in his shoulder seemed to be lessening. Funny what a new mission could do for you.

But his newfound sense of self hadn't prepared him for what he thought he was facing. Should he just walk away, give her time to compose herself, and come back in a while? Pretend he hadn't observed this? Except, what had he actually observed? Her hand moving beneath the covers? She could just be adjusting the blanket.

He stood there a minute, waiting for her to finish waking up. While she'd been sleeping, he'd spent a few minutes doing his shoulder workout, Bailey sitting there and watching with a somber, chiding look for him having waited so long to get with the program. Then he took a long walk outside with Bailey, who'd apparently decided guarding the place was his new main goal in life. He ran ahead then checked the perimeter before returning to walk next to Wolf.

"No bombs, big guy, but the bad guys could be hiding out there. Just keep it up."

Wolf's .45 was in the holster on his hip, and he

carried his rifle in his hand, ready to aim and shoot at a moment's notice. He was no longer the sharpshooter he once had been, damn the fucking shoulder, but he'd practiced enough that he was confident in his ability to take down anything around here.

Alex had told him the property was about three acres, most of it running back from the house. It was pretty open, but there were clusters of trees here and there someone could hide in. It bothered him that the place wasn't fenced, but there were big floodlights he planned on keeping on at all times plus some warning sensors tied into the security system.

Of course, he'd had enough experience to know that if someone really wanted to attack them, they could find a way. No one was more devious than the bad guys they fought in Iraq and Afghanistan. He'd just have to be very alert.

But now he really wanted a look at Lacey's wound, which the nurse had told him should be checked on a regular basis. He probably should change the dressing and check for infection. The instructions from the hospital said she should be seen by a doctor in seven days. He'd have to talk to Alex about how they'd manage that.

Her arm might need icing again, and she also should probably take another pain pill. Something over the counter at the very least. Alex's incredible wife had stocked some, along with the groceries and just about anything else they could need or want.

He waited another moment, trying to decide if he

should wake her, or would she be embarrassed if he'd actually seen—No! He had to get that out of his mind. Especially if she'd been doing what he thought, because he really wanted it to be his hand between her warm thighs, stroking and caressing her, bringing her to climax and...

For fuck's sake, Wolf! Get a grip. Fucking her brains out is not on your to-do list.

At that moment, she shifted slightly, her eyes opened, and she looked over at him. "Um, hi."

"Hi." *Sparkling, Wolf.* "Just wanted to check on you. Remember, the doctor wanted me to monitor your arm, plus I wanted to see if you needed another pain pill. And it's time for the antibiotic. Kujo dropped off all your meds."

"Oh." She moved her arm a little. "Okay on the one but not the other. Not right now. I've a pretty high pain threshold, and I don't like the way they make me feel. I'd rather try ice again if I need something. Um, have you been standing there a long time?"

Don't say yes.

"No. Just a few seconds." Was that relief on her face? "I checked on you a couple of times, but you were out like a light. You needed the rest. You've been through a lot."

He watched as she closed her eyes for a moment again then opened them and managed to push herself to a sitting position using her good arm and hand. He tried his best to ignore the sharp flash of pain across her face. Wolf wanted to offer her help, but he wasn't sure exactly what lines he could cross and what would seem invasive.

"I was told Alex's wife had unpacked my clothes?"

Wolf nodded. "They're in the dresser over there."

"Good. I'd like to wear something besides these scrubs." She paused and nibbled her lower lip, the sight making his cock twitch. "I think I can handle getting dressed."

"Oh, sure." He pushed himself away from the doorjamb. "Just let me know if you need help, and I mean that in the most utilitarian way."

She stared at him then burst out laughing. "I guess we're going to have to figure some things out here. It's only my arm that's injured, but it makes a lot of things difficult. I may need help with stuff that could be uncomfortable for both of us if we let it."

He cleared his throat. "So, what do you suggest?"

She blew out a breath. "I suggest I not be a pain in the ass about it and that you pretend it's just stuff you do every day."

He burst out laughing. He couldn't help it. And it broke the tension that had stretched between them.

"I can handle that. Lord knows. I've been a hermit for so long, my people skills need a lot of work, but I'll make a real effort."

Her smile eased the tension riding him. "Good. And I'll try to do the same."

He studied her, curiosity stamped on his face. "I

don't think you've been hiding from life though." A pause. "Have you?"

"I guess not." Curiosity bloomed in her eyes. "Should I ask what you've been hiding from?"

"Not yet. Okay?" No, he damn well wasn't going to tell her what had locked him away from the world for six months.

"Let's work on getting you into real clothes. Need help?"

"Let me see." She managed to swing her legs over the side of the bed and push herself to her feet. Then, she must have realized she was standing there in just panties and the oversized top.

Bailey had come to stand beside him and made a little mewling sound in his throat.

Lacey chuckled. "Is he going to help me, too?"

"If you let him. Maybe he'll do a better job than I can."

"How about letting me give it a try myself. If I need help, I promise to ask for it. Can you, um, just step outside the room for a minute?"

No, I want to see you in just your T-shirt and little panties.

"Okay. But please holler if you have a problem. I promise not to look."

She actually laughed. "That would make it kinda hard to help, right? But I promise I'll yell if I need either you or Bailey."

He left the door open but moved to the side, Bailey sitting expectantly next to him.

"Yeah, buddy. This could be a problem. I have to keep reminding myself she's my responsibility and that Alex Rossi would kill me if I took advantage of it. Right?"

Bailey made that little sound in his throat and leaned against Wolf's leg.

"Okay, I can tell you like her, too, kiddo. That's good, because if you didn't, we'd be in a hell of a fix."

He stood there, willing the images that flooded his mind to go away. He could hear the signs of her moving and tried not to think what she was doing, like getting clothes, trying to pull them on. Or wonder if she'd really been bringing herself to orgasm and what had triggered it. Just when he was ready to chance it and see if she had a problem, she called out to him.

"Wolf?"

"Yes? Need help?"

"Much as I hate to admit, I do."

Okay, then.

He eased around the doorway and into the room, Bailey right beside him. Lacey was sitting on the edge of the bed, both feet shoved into a pair of jeans, but they were only pulled partway up her legs. A top lay next to her on the bed. Frustration was all over her face.

"I thought I could just pull them up." She shook her head. "Harder than I thought. It's tough to balance, and I didn't want to chance falling down."

"Good decision. No problem. We'll just get it done."

"And I have another problem. I can't lift and stretch my arms, so I can't take this top off and pull on another one.

"Okay. Let's make it happen." He was really testing his self-control.

Bailey followed him into the room and stopped right beside Lacey. As if he'd understood what Wolf said, Bailey moved even closer and nudged her with his nose.

She giggled. "I think he wants to help, too."

"Too bad." Wolf managed a grin. "This is my responsibility."

He decided on the jeans first, holding his breath when his fingers brushed the outside of her thighs. It took a little doing, but he managed it without too much skin-to-skin contact, although he couldn't stop himself from admiring how smooth that skin was or how nice her thighs were. Maybe denying himself sex for so long was backfiring now, but he had a feeling it had more to do with Lacey than with his self-deprivation. He forced himself to concentrate on the task at hand and not how much he wanted to run his fingers over her curves or string kisses along that delicate skin.

Then he picked up the blouse lying on the bed next to her.

"Okay." She blew out a breath. "I'll just pretend this is happening to someone else. It hurts to raise my left arm, so getting this scrubs top off first is a priority. Then we have to get this one"—she indicated the blouse next to her "on me."

He managed a little grin.

"I'll just treat it like a mission. Hold on."

He reached into his pocket and pulled out an all-purpose knife. With efficient motions, he sliced the scrubs top open from her neck to her waist, doing his best to ignore the lush breasts that suddenly came into view.

Jesus!

Reaching over her, he cut another slice down the back of the fabric then slid one remnant down each arm. He was very careful not to bump her wound as he did it, but holy shit! She sat there naked from the waist up, and he had a very difficult time not looking at her nicely rounded breasts with their dark rosy tips.

His cock twitched in response.

Oh god, kill me now.

To her credit, she just sat there, immobile, not trying to hide herself but also not looking at him. He picked up the other top, relieved to see it buttoned up the front. With minimum pain to her injured arm, he managed to slip it on and button it up. He wondered if she noticed how his fingers shook when his knuckles collided with her breasts.

He thanked god she seemed to be avoiding a comment on it like he was.

Then, finally, she was dressed, and he helped her to stand.

"I think I'm exhausted." A tiny giggle drifted from her mouth.

"Want to lie down again?"

She shook her head. "No, I want to take that pill and sit down someplace besides this bedroom. It makes me feel like I'm still in the hospital."

"Time for the antibiotic, too," he reminded her.

Once she was up, he let her balance on his arms while she slipped her feet into her shoes. When she looked up at him, their faces were scant inches apart. He nearly got lost in her eyes, a deep blue, almost navy, with thick dark lashes. He noticed an enticing smattering of freckles on her cheeks and the sweet fullness of her lips.

She was still gripping his arms, still staring up at him, as if they were both glued to the floor, and he seemed unable to breathe. More than anything, he wanted to kiss those lips, to run his tongue over them. To touch her everywhere. Well, damn! Could he possibly be more inappropriate?

"There." She let out a slow breath. "You wouldn't think a little wound in my arm would make things so difficult."

"I'll bet it hurts like a mother—" He stopped himself. "Like a real bitch. Will you let me check it and make sure nothing bad's happening?"

"Yes. Although I hate this whole thing. Not you,"

she added quickly. "Just the whole situation with the wound. I'm not used to depending on other people."

"Maybe this is Fate's way of telling you it's okay," he pointed out. "I'm guessing you aren't used to relying on other people."

"No." She sighed. "It's just been Heather and me for so long, since our parents were killed in a plane crash. We didn't have much in the way of family to reach out to, so we each developed our own careers and built our own lives. And we've never gone this long without contacting each other." She gave a hiccuppy little laugh. "I used to tell her Trace would wonder if he was marrying both sisters."

That made his brain take a little twist.

"Was he jealous of that? Do you think he might have killed her in a fit of rage and hidden the body?"

She laughed, a real one this time. "Oh, no. Trace loved—*loves*—her beyond anything. And we both did our best to always make sure he knew he came first with her. No, no, no. He worshiped her. In fact, the last time I talked to both of them, which was two weeks ago, he wanted me to come out here and spend a couple of days with them. He said I could get some great pictures."

Still, Wolf filed that little tidbit away to share with the sheriff.

"Okay, let's check that arm."

He eased her back down to the edge of the bed and gently probed the area the bandage covered. It didn't feel hot to him, which was good. No infection.

But it was time for her to take her meds, get her bandaged changed, and maybe use the ice again.

"I think I'd like to brush my teeth first," she told him. "My mouth still tastes like the hospital."

"Okay. Then we'll do the medication, the bandage, and maybe some ice. I like that Alex's wife got the kind you can wrap around your arm."

"Thank you."

"And how about a late lunch after that? You haven't eaten a thing except that tea and toast since this morning, and that's not good for you, especially with the meds."

"You're right, it isn't. But what about you?"

"Lunch would be good for both of us, especially before you take another pill. I set something up outside. I hope that's okay. There's furniture on the porch, it's warm, and the view is great."

"Sounds good. Thank you so much. For everything."

They both avoided the subject of his assistance with her clothes.

"My pleasure. Really. It's been a long time since I've done anything I actually enjoyed. Now, come on. Sit down, and I'll get a pillow to prop your arm."

He hoped the scene in the backyard would relax her because right at that moment, Alex was holding a meeting at the small library in Eagle Rock to set up a large search and rescue operation. He hoped something positive would come from it. Maybe there might even be someone at the meeting whose memory was jogged. Who'd remember something they brushed off as inconsequential but now realized might be a clue as to the whereabouts of the missing couple.

∼

Hunter sat in the back of the room, listening to the sheriff describe the situation and what he wanted from the people there.

"This couple has been missing for two weeks," Rossi told them. "Now I know people disappear in the Crazies, and unless we have specifics about where and when, we've rarely been able to find them. But there are things about this that make it different."

"Like what?" someone shouted.

"For one thing, the missing woman's sister was on her way to meet with me yesterday when she was shot."

"Shot?" the same voice cried out.

Then the word flowed through the crowd, like water rumbling over the sand. Hunter could feel the tension begin to seep through the room.

"Shot?"

"Did he say shot?"

"Someone was shot?"

"Is she dead?"

"Dead? Did he say dead?"

"Hold it, please." Rossi held up his hand. "Let's

take it easy here. We won't get anywhere if we panic. No, the woman is not dead."

I might be better off if she was, Hunter thought. Only Alex Rossi had proven to be a dog after a bone and, if he had a dead body, he'd never let it go. At least, if he couldn't find this woman and her fiancé, eventually he'd have to give up. And he, obsessive person that he was, planned to make sure there was no way Rossi could ever find out what happened to the couple. When Alex Rossi took over as sheriff, he'd destroyed the fun they'd had going for ten years, bastard that he was. They'd had to find something else to get their blood going.

It had taken a while, but The Hunt had turned out to be a perfect solution. It was exciting, challenging, dangerous—all the things they needed to attain the highest level of pleasure. He'd be damned if he'd let a bunch of outsiders destroy it.

But he'd have to be careful. Convince Rossi he was the best person to scour his own area.

"Do you know who shot her?" someone asked.

"Not yet," Rossi told them. "But we did recover the bullet from the wound, so when we find the gun, we can match it. And we do know what kind of gun it is. My office will be contacting the Montana State Police and the courts to see what kind of search can be instituted."

They'll never be able to do that.

Hunter was damn sure of that, no matter how bold and assured Alex Rossi sounded. He had used an old hunting rifle that he kept more for sentimental reasons. It was in his closet, broken down, and when he got home, he planned to ride to a far corner of the ranch and bury it.

Hunter was well aware of the legalities involved in that kind of search, of how long it would take to push the requests through the courts, especially when there was not one shred of proof pointing to anyone at the moment. But the fact that the man would be rattling a lot of cages was annoying. He couldn't decide if they should finish off the latest prey or prolong the situation, since it would probably be some time before they could "gather" another "target."

"Do you have an actual count of how many people have disappeared over, say, the past ten years?" another person asked.

Rossi shook his head. "Not actual, because we don't have good records, sad to say. Plus, some of the people reported as missing eventually turned up."

A man sitting close to the front raised his hand. "Where were they? Had they gotten lost?"

Rossi nodded. "Some of them. It's hard to find your way out of the Crazies if you lose your direction."

"What about cell phones. Couldn't they call?"

Rossi shrugged. "You know as well as I do reception is spotty there, especially if you're in one of the caves."

One of the men up front nodded his head. "We nearly lost another couple last year because of that."

The sheriff lifted a sheet of paper from the top of the stack he had with him.

"I've put together a flyer with a list of things to watch for, so if you see strangers, you can note where they are and let me know. Grab some before you leave. My deputies and I will be dropping stacks of these off at the various campgrounds and motels and gas stations in the county, and the state police have agreed to help paper the rest of the state."

"That's good," a woman down front commented.

"We have no idea how many of the people who disappeared just got permanently lost somehow or met with what we'll call for now misadventure. We need to be a lot smarter about this. We want people to love Montana, to love vacationing in and around the Crazy Mountains. For that to happen, we have to find out what happened to Heather Cooper and her fiancé and then backtrack on other disappearances."

"So, what can we do in the meantime?" one of the men asked.

"We're organizing search parties," Rossi told him. "I have people trained in this who spent the morning dividing this entire area into search grids. You all know most of my deputies are former SEALs and have been trained to hunt for people, but we're just a very small group. I'd like as many of you as possible to sign up for one of the teams. We're not just looking for people wandering around lost but also, unfortunately, for bodies, for signs of abduction, for anything that looks out of place."

And I'll be sure to keep them as far away from the target as possible.

A man in a plaid shirt and Stetson stood up and looked around the room. Josh Farraday, Hunter noted. Fuck. That guy was like a dog after a bone with everything he did. He'd like to shoot the asshole and bury him where he'd never be found, but that would only create more problems. He was the kind who could stumble over what was happening by accident, and that couldn't happen.

"The ranchers association is behind this all the way, Sheriff. We'll get as many members as possible to sign up and also provide any other help we can. If I can take a stack of those flyers, we'll help you get them distributed."

Hunter stepped forward. "I'm happy to lead one of the search teams. Just tell me what to look for so I know I'm doing it right."

And so I can mislead as many people as possible.

Alex Rossi nodded at him. "Thanks. I really appreciate it." He looked around the room. "Most of you here know as much about the land as anyone can, so your participation is a big help. My deputy Zane Halstead, who many of you know, is set up at this table here with signup sheets. If those of you who are able to would go ahead and put your names in, there are starting spots for each team." He looked at his watch. "I'd like to get as much ground covered today as possible."

As he moved up to get in line, Hunter made sure to stop and greet other people he knew, exchanging comments with them.

"Glad you're doing this," one man told him. "You know the Crazies as well as anyone."

And can misdirect the search better because of it.

"Happy to help." He shook his head. "Terrible, terrible thing."

He hung around a while longer, on the surface, appearing to chat with different people he knew. But he really was keeping an eye on the people who sought Rossi out and were talking to him earnestly. Had they seen the couple Hunter liked to call The Prey and were telling the sheriff about it? Had anyone seen the others who were part of his game and disappeared because of it?

He and his partner needed to be extremely careful. They'd taken great care in selecting their prey and setting up The Hunt. They'd been damn fucking lucky not to get scooped up when Alex Rossi came in and destroyed the nice little thing they had going with the young flesh around here. They'd had to be real careful setting up this new activity, and he wasn't about to let some smart-ass destroy it.

Leading a search team would not only allow him to keep an eye on things but to misdirect people. Why the fuck had that damned woman shown up anyway?

He had started toward the door when Alex Rossi stopped him.

"Thanks again for offering to lead one of the teams."

"Happy to do it. I hate the thought of anyone being lost out there and not able to get back. Terrible way to die."

"That it is. And you know more about this entire county, I think, than anyone else, so your knowledge will be valuable."

"Thank you for that."

"We'll text you a list of people in your area you could contact, but I'm sure you have some you think would do a good job. Get hold of them and get started right away. We don't have time to waste."

"I will. My family's been here for three generations, so I've got a pretty good handle on who would be the best for this. And I'm anxious to get started."

Sheriff Rossi fake-smiled him and shook his hand. The sooner he got away from him the better. He had some prep work to do before he could start any kind of search. But one thing was sure. He wasn't leading anyone to the missing couple. Not even to their bodies, if that turned out to be all that was left of them.

He ended the conversation without being too obvious that was what he was doing. Sheriff Alex Rossi made his skin itch.

By the time he left and headed for his truck, he'd figured out those he wanted on his search team, people who could be nudged in the right direction—or away from the wrong one. And the names he'd take from Rossi's suggestions that could be easily manipulated. He just hoped to hell they could get this over with sooner rather than later.

Despite himself, though, he was looking forward to the night's adventure. If they had to cool it for a while, he wanted to extend this one as long as possible, until he was forced to get rid of them or lose everything.

CHAPTER 8

LACEY WANTED to cry when she saw what Wolf had set up for their late lunch or whatever the meal was. There was a small round table and two chairs on the back porch, and he'd set out two plates with sandwiches and fruit. She could have sobbed at his thoughtfulness when she saw he'd cut her sandwiches into small triangles and her fruit into individual bite-size pieces.

"I wasn't sure how much you could use your arm," he said, avoiding her eyes, "and I wanted to make it as easy as possible for you."

She couldn't remember the last time a man had treated her with such thoughtfulness, which certainly didn't say a lot for the men she'd dated.

"I, uh, remember what it was like when my shoulder got shot up. Just raising my hand to my mouth was a motherf—bast—uh, bitch."

Lacey laughed. She couldn't help it.

"Cursing doesn't offend me, Wolf. Just be yourself." Then her smile disappeared. "I'm sorry about your shoulder. Do you want to tell me about it?"

Did he? He could hardly stand to deal with it himself. He certainly didn't need her pity, not when he was trying to establish a new life for himself here. He didn't want people to think Alex was hiring a cripple.

He shook his head. "Not now. Let's focus on your injury, okay?"

He pulled out a chair for her, and as soon as she sat down, Bailey planted himself next to her.

"I'm telling you, he never does that." Wolf shook his head. "I don't know about this. He's been a one-person dog up to now." Then he smiled at her, and it transformed his face. "But I might be willing to share him with you."

"That…would be nice."

"Business first," he told her, handing her a glass of water and a pill he dug from a vial in his pocket. "If you're a good girl, you can have dessert. That Micki Rossi thought of everything."

"I can't wait to meet her. Except I'm sure I'll be jealous of the wonder woman. What's she like?"

"I have no idea. I haven't met her yet." When she just stared at him, he laughed. "Lacey, I got here about the same time you got shot off the road. I know nothing."

"You all sure move fast." She swallowed the pill

then held her arm still while he wrapped the ice around it followed by a cloth bandage.

"Think you're ready to eat now?" he asked.

She nodded, discovering to her surprise that she actually was. She waited until Wolf was seated across from her before picking up the first small triangle of her sandwich. "Thank you for this."

He nodded, staring at her. "Are they okay? You can handle them?"

"Yes, and I'm impressed. Very neat and precise."

"It's all that military training." He winked, something she was sure was a rare gesture from him. "Now. Let's eat some lunch. Maybe by the time we're finished, Alex will be done with his search and rescue meeting. He said he'd stop by and fill us in."

"Do you think he'll get a lot of people to sign up?"

Wolf shrugged. "I have no idea what people around here are like, although, if Alex and Zane and the others are an example, I'd say you'll get at least a decent number of volunteers."

They ate for a while in silence. She found she wasn't all that hungry, but she forced herself to eat, knowing if she made herself sick, she'd just be a burden to everyone. Especially to Wolf, who had gotten stuck with the role of nursemaid.

"Listen to me." He set his fork down. "I'm not stuck with anything."

"Oh my god. Did I actually say that out loud?"

"I'm glad you did so we can clear this up. I'm glad the sheriff assigned me to your protective detail."

Her laugh had a slightly hysterical edge to it. "A detail that consists of one man. You. With no relief in sight."

He took her hand in one of his big ones. "I'm exactly where I want to be. This is the first time in months I've actually felt as if I still have a purpose in life. I'm not kidding. So please don't think this is any kind of a chore."

"You know, I must have talked to a hundred people in this area, trying to get a lead in what happened to Heather and Trace. They all looked at me like I was crazy, telling me people got lost in the Crazies all the time and never got found. I can't believe people aren't still looking for them."

"Maybe they are and they just don't talk about it. Were your sister and her fiancé the type to explore dangerous places?"

"No." She shook her head. "They loved to go camping. They knew all the rules, the what to do and what not to do. And they'd never do anything to put themselves in that kind of danger."

"So they're experienced at this."

"Yes. Which is why I can't believe they'd go into any area where they'd learned people had gotten lost and never been found."

Suddenly all the emotion she'd been bottling up, the fear, the uncertainty, the terror came bursting through her. Tears burned her eyes, and she did her best to blink them back but it seemed to be an unstoppable force. She'd kept it together ever since

Heather and Trace disappeared, but now everything from the past few weeks just exploded. Tears ran down her face, and her shoulders shook with the force of the emotion. She tried to blot her face with the napkin, but the tears would not stop. She bent over with the force of the emotion, resting her forehead on her good arm as the tears continued to flow.

"Lacey?"

She heard Wolf's voice as if from a great distance, but she didn't have breath to answer him. The feelings of devastation and disaster gripped her like a vise.

"Lacey," he repeated. "Can you talk to me? What can I do for you?"

She thought she heard him cursing under his breath and wished she could pull herself together, but all the discipline she'd needed since the disappearance seemed to disappear and leave her a bawling mess.

She sensed movement then she was gently lifted from her chair and, in seconds, found herself on Wolf's lap with his arms cradling her. If her common sense had been present at all she never would have leaned into him, but the hard wall of his chest and the strength of his arms around gave her comfort she sorely needed. She was vaguely aware he held her so her injured arm wasn't getting any pressure, and that his long fingers were stroking her hair.

She had no idea how long they sat there like that until at last, the torrent of tears dried up and her hiccupping sobs subsided. Finally, she was able to lift her head and draw a breath.

"I'm so sorry." She reached for her napkin to blot her face. "You must think I'm an idiot."

"I think you are an extremely brave woman who is terrified about what might have happened to her family and has had nothing but doors slammed in her face. That about right?"

She hiccupped again. "Yes, but—"

"But nothing." He guided her head to his shoulder again. "I think it's a miracle you've held it together this long. And getting shot sure didn't help."

Bailey had come to sit beside them, resting his head on Lacey's thigh.

"I think he's trying to take my place," Wolf joked.

Lacey knew she should move, should ease herself off his lap and back into her chair, but he was so solid, and she felt such security sitting here. Finally she lifted her head to look at him and discovered her face was a millimeter from his. Long lashes couldn't mask the heat blazing in his eyes, and neither her discomfort nor the effects of her meds could prevent her from feeling the thick shaft of his cock pressing into her bottom.

She thought about shifting but figured that would only make things worse. She tried to pretend it wasn't happening, but that was like trying to pretend her face wasn't splotchy from tears. Oh god! What the hell should she do? What the hell was going through his mind.

She was sitting there trying to make her muddled mind work when Wolf cleared his throat.

"Uh, I think I should probably lift you back into your chair. I mean, if you're okay."

She managed a tiny laugh. "I'm not sure what I am, but I agree with you."

But he didn't move, didn't shift her at all, just held her on his lap. Then, tentatively, he put two fingers beneath her chin and tilted up her face.

"Don't look." She refused to look at him. "I'm a mess."

"What you are is a beautiful woman in a desperate situation who's worried sick about her family and trying to recover after being shot. I haven't known you long, but I have nothing but admiration for you. I told the sheriff if anything ever happened to me, you're the one I'd want looking for answers. But you put yourself in terrible danger doing it."

"I know. I certainly didn't expect it. I had it in my mind that they had gotten lost in one of the caves or something and people were too inconsiderate to keep looking." She studied his face. "But it's more than that, isn't it?"

"I'd like to tell you no but I can't." He lifted a hand in a tentative gesture and very slowly stroked her damp cheek with his fingers. "Lacey, I—" He stopped, shook his head, and let out a slow breath. "Listen. I'm not sure how to say this—"

She held up a hand. "I feel it, too. Is it crazy? We don't even know each other, but I feel…something powerful." She shook her head. "I think I'm embarrassing myself."

"No. You're not." He let out a sigh. "You have no idea what a fucked-up mess I am. I've been hiding from the world. I haven't even had anything resembling a date in way too many months. And I'm probably way out of line here, but—"

She touched his mouth with the tips of her fingers. "And I'm a big mess here, too. So why don't you just shut up and kiss me."

She didn't know who was more startled, her for saying the words or Wolf when he heard them. But he shifted her slightly in his lap, mindful of her wounded arm, cupped her chin, and slowly lowered his mouth to hers. The contact was so electric, it shot through her entire body. Her nerves sizzled, and her blood heated, even as her brain tried to tell her she shouldn't be doing this.

Wolf caressed her lips with his tongue, running the tip along the seam while holding her head in place with one large hand. When he nudged her mouth gently, she opened for him, and his tongue thrust inside. Heat consumed her, flashing through her body. Her nipples hardened into tight peaks and, between her thighs, the folds of her sex were wet and throbbing.

Holy crap!

What was going on here?

A little voice whispered in her ear that she was getting herself into trouble, but she didn't care. None of the men she'd been with had ever elicited a response like this from her, certainly not with just kissing. So, as his tongue plundered her mouth, bringing every nerve to life, she just hung on for the ride.

She had no idea how long the kiss went on, only that every part of her body seemed to respond to it. And what did that say about her choices in men when a physically and emotionally damaged former SEAL turned her on more than anyone else. Ever.

At last, Wolf lifted his mouth from hers but only a fraction. Their faces were so close, she could count his eyelashes. Fire burned in his coffee-colored eyes, and his breathing was as irregular as hers.

"I don't know if I should tell you that's the best thing that's happened to me in too long a time or apologize for taking advantage of you."

Lacey let out a slow breath. "I vote for the first one. And there was no taking advantage. What are we doing here, Wolf?"

"I don't think I have an answer to that. Lacey, I'm sure I'm out of line here. You're—"

She lifted her hand to touch his mouth and, as she did, she bumped her bad arm. "Ouch."

"See?" He shook his head. "Damn. I should be shot."

She studied his face. "There are two of us here."

"But—"

"No buts. Okay?"

She was conscious of the care he took as he lifted

her from his lap and settled her in the chair she'd been seated in before.

"I'm supposed to be protecting you. Maybe that means from me, too."

"Stop." She shook her head. "It was me, too." She grinned. "And worth a little bit of pain."

"Lacey." He blew out a long breath. "I don't even know where to begin here. My life has been—"

She reached up with her good hand and touched his lips. "I don't want to hear it. No apologies. Everyone's life has some kinks in it. Some more than others. Wolf, everyone carries baggage."

"But mine is damn fucking heavy," he burst out.

"And tonight, if you want, we can sit out here and kill a bottle of wine, and you can tell me all about it. But right now, could I please just enjoy the best thing that's happened to me in forever?"

He blew out a breath. "Okay. Okay." He paused. "For now. And I think—"

At that moment, someone began knocking on the front door. Wolf rose from his chair.

"I'll get it. It's probably Alex, come to tell us how the meeting went." He paused a moment then quickly brushed a light kiss over her lips, as if he might change his mind. Or she would. "Be right back."

She had mostly composed herself when Wolf came back out on the porch with Alex following him.

"If you've got another glass, I'll take some of that iced tea," the sheriff said, sitting down with them.

"I'll get it." Wolf head back into the kitchen.

"How are you doing?"

Lacey tried not to squirm under Alex's piercing gaze. Did what they'd just done show on her face? Would the sheriff decide someone else should be her keeper?

"Doing okay. Only took one pain pill today. I'm trying not to use too many of them. They make me loopy."

"I hear you, but don't push yourself too hard. Don't get to the point where the pain exceeds your ability to deal with it."

"I won't."

"You and Wolf getting along okay?" He studied her face. "Everything all right?"

She nodded. "Yes, and yes."

"Listen, Lacey. I only just met Wolf the day you got shot, so I don't know much about him, but I like to think I'm a good judge of character. I have good feelings about him and not just because he's a SEAL. But if…"

Lacey tried not to laugh. "Everything is fine. Better than fine. He's exactly what you think he is, and he's bending over backward to take good care of me. It's kind of an awkward situation, but he's excelling at it."

No kidding.

"Okay. I'll take your word for it. I'd hate to think I was wrong about him."

"No, you're not. I promise I would tell you if you were."

He had barely finished speaking when Wolf came back onto the porch carrying a glass. He filled it and handed it to Alex.

"So." He took a long drink of the cool liquid. "Interesting meeting."

"In what way?" Wolf asked.

He had eased his chair closer to Lacey and draped his arm over the back of it. She was shocked at how good she felt about it. She saw Alex look from one to the other, and a hint of a smile teased at his mouth, but he didn't say anything.

"Okay, details about the meeting," Wolf said. "Anybody there give off strange vibes?"

"More than I'd like." Alex frowned. "But not necessarily because of this. I learned from day one that this area has a lot of secrets. I'm still navigating my way through them."

"Was Cordell Ritchie there?"

Alex nodded. "You know, I keep trying to figure that guy out. He's a big deal in the ranchers association. Been here a long time and has one of the biggest spreads. About forty-five hundred acres. Of course, he also runs one of the biggest herds of cattle."

Wolf frowned. "I sense some kind of hesitancy here. What's up?"

Alex took a long swallow of his iced tea and set the glass down.

"Okay, here's the deal. Remember I just sort of mentioned a situation when I arrived here, about some of the rich assholes raping underage girls?"

Wolf nodded. "Makes me sick."

"Well, there was a lot more to it than that. The men were all very, very wealthy ranchers who apparently got together after a party one night and decided to play a little game. Individually, they would select a target. Then, at a party at the girl's home or some other event, get them alone in the bedroom, rape them, and promise to kill them if they told anyone."

Lacey stared at the sheriff, nausea bubbling up in her throat.

"The girls believed them, I'm sure."

"They did." Alex nodded. "Especially after a couple of them reported the rape to the sheriff, who killed them on orders from these guys."

Now Lacey was sure she was going to be sick. She gripped the arms of her chair as dizziness swept over her.

"Hold everything." Wolf hurried into the kitchen and returned with a dish towel soaked in cold water. He held it to Lacey's forehead, watching her carefully. "You aren't going to throw up or anything, are you? I mean it's okay, if you need to. I just wanted a little warning."

"I'm good," she finally said and smiled at him. "Thanks."

Wolf dropped into the chair next to her again, rage carving lines in his face. "What happened to the men?"

"During my investigation of the murders, we managed to root out several others. We even had some of the girls come forward once we could assure them of anonymity. We knew they'd never have to testify in court because none of the men we arrested wanted the publicity of a trial.

"Alex, I can't believe these men got away with it. Who killed the girls?"

"The former sheriff, an asshole piece of shit name Jeff Bartell. He's rotting away in prison as we speak."

A muscle twitched in Wolf's jaw. "It wasn't gang rape, was it?"

"No." Alex shook his head. "They were smart enough to stay away from that. They selected their quarry individually but certainly bragged about it to each other. But it occurred to me that there might still be ranchers out there who weren't caught, for whatever reason. They might have dodged a bullet that time, but it didn't kill their need for excitement. They needed a new hobby and I'm sure were looking for something to get their blood racing. And maybe killing unsuspecting tourists was what they came up with."

"You mean...just murdering people for fun?"

"No, not just plain murder. That wouldn't be enough to give them the charge they wanted. That thrill they were missing. But something with a sharp edge of danger to it. I just don't know what it is yet."

"But..." Lacey stared at one then the other. "But that makes me sick."

"Right there with you," Alex told her.

"Scum like that need to be eradicated in a very

painful manner." Wolf spat the words out like sharp knives.

"I agree. Thing is, we have to figure out how they'd do it, what they'd do, and how they'd get away with it."

Lacey leaned forward. "Did you get any impressions of anyone at the meeting? Someone who seemed off-kilter or anything?"

Alex shrugged. "I've been trying to analyze it. There are a lot of nice people in this area. We also have our fair share of assholes but, other than the rapes, I haven't had trouble with them. And that chapter is closed, thank god. I just have to deal with their arrogance. Some of the ranching families have been here for generations. They have enough money to buy the whole mountain range, and some of them think they can live by their own rules."

"That's got to be a real pain."

"In more ways than one." He looked down at his hands as if trying to decide to tell him something. "My father-in-law, Micki's dad, was…one of the men involved."

"What?" Wolf stared at the man. "Are you shitting me?"

"I wish." He rubbed a hand over his face. "Micki and I met when she came back here for her dad's birthday party, and someone poisoned him. It seems he was about to blow the whistle on their outrageous game, and they wanted to prevent it."

Lacey's head was spinning. "But...but that all seems so outrageous and unbelievable."

"No kidding. Anyway, finding his killer had me spending a lot of time with Micki, and here we are. But being married to her also gives me a foothold in the elite ranching community. I think that will be a big help finding out what's going on and discovering where your family is, Lacey."

"None of my business," Wolf interjected, "but that whole situation must have been hell on Micki."

The muscles in Alex's face tightened, and anger flashed for a moment in his eyes.

"It nearly destroyed her." His jaw tightened. "She's a very strong woman, though, and ended up staying here, thank god, and building a life with me. Her mother, however, ended up moving out of state, and her brother doesn't live here anymore, either. They sold the ranch, and Micki uses her share of the profits to do stuff like this house."

"She sounds like quite a woman," Lacey said in a soft voice. She could hardly imagine going through a nightmare like that.

"She is. She's really anxious to meet you, but her job's got her tied up right now."

"What does she do?" Lacey wondered what kind of work a woman like that did.

Alex smiled. "She's an assistant county prosecutor. They give her the toughest cases because she goes after the guilty like a feral dog."

"Be sure and tell her we thank her for taking the time to get this house set up."

"I will. Meanwhile, back to the crisis at hand."

"Yeah," Wolf reminded him. "You were about to give us a rundown on any vibes from the meeting that bothered you."

Alex ran his fingers through his hair.

"I have to say, for the most part, the people in this county are decent citizens. Oh, we always have a few bad apples, but you get that anywhere. But they weren't who I was looking for. I was mostly looking at the ranchers. The ones who I always wondered about when I think back to that horrendous tragedy."

"I can't even imagine," Lacey told him. "What a nightmare to live through."

"So what you're suggesting," Wolf said, "is that you got hinky vibes from some of the ranchers who might have been part of the rape tragedy, but there was nothing pointing to them, so they got off scot-free."

"I am. Some more than others. There's just something about the attitude of a few of them. A touch of arrogance that makes me itch."

Wolf frowned. "Like who?"

"Well, like Cordell Ritchie, for example."

"Wait." Lacey shifted in her chair, being careful of her arm, which had started to throb again. "Do you remember I told you about Cordell Ritchie? About how he approached me when I was gassing up, introduced himself, and said he'd like to help?"

"I'll bet he would," Alex snorted, "if he's caught up in this."

"But involved in what?" Wolf wanted to know. "Would he and his friends be killing visitors for sport? Is the hunting season that bad? What's their deal?"

Alex grimaced. "Chalk it up to boredom, humungous egos, and a total disrespect for other people. What other kind of people rape young girls for the thrill of it? But ever since I spoke to you, Lacey, something's been digging at the back of my mind. Zane and I are putting together our own search and rescue team. I'm also heading right now to meet with Hank Patterson and get his Brotherhood Protectors involved. Hank knows this area better than the back of his hand, and all his men are former military. Lacey, we'll find your sister and her fiancé, no matter what. Count on it."

She was almost afraid to do that. "Ever since I got here, and no one seemed to give me much hope, I've been battling the fear they're dead. But if they're not, where are they?"

"That's what I'm going to find out," Alex assured her. "Well, I'll let you both get back to finishing your meal, but I promise either Zane or I will report in regularly. Somewhere, somehow, your sister and her fiancé tripped a switch, and we're going to find it."

"I don't know how to thank you, Sheriff."

"Alex, please. And you can thank me by

convincing your bodyguard to make this a permanent gig."

"But you hardly know me," Wolf protested.

"Maybe, but I do know my gut instincts, and I haven't been wrong yet. I'll show myself out. You take care of our guest."

Guest. Lacey almost laughed at that one.

"That's the plan," he told the sheriff.

"Listen, I'm going to check how the SAR organization is going. I want the teams to get going ASAP. My gut tells me this is more than just lost campers and I have a greater sense of urgency. I want to talk to Hank Patterson and get his input on everything. He's sending a team from Brotherhood Protectors and he'll have a good handle on the situation. He knows this place inside and out. He's the one who got me into this job and I trust him more than almost anyone else, except my own people."

"Please thank him for me," Lacey told him.

"No thanks necessary. It's what we do. When I have more information, I'll come back here and we can see exactly where we are and what we need to do. I have some ideas, but they might sound farfetched right now. I'll call you later."

Lacey hadn't realized how exhausted she was until she heard the front door close. She slumped in her chair, feeling as if all the energy had drained out of her, plus her arm had begun to throb again.

"I can't believe this." She managed a sip of iced tea. "I feel as if I just got up, and I'm ready for bed again."

"You've had an experience that would flatten most people," Wolf pointed out. "You were run off the road, shot, had surgery. Damn, Lacey. That would knock anyone on their ass."

"Oh, good. I don't feel like such a wimp."

"No wimp, but maybe another little lie-down wouldn't hurt. I know you want to be in the meeting with Alex and the others, so some rest would do you some good."

She smiled at the concern in his face.

"Thank you."

Wolf pulled her chair back. "Anyway, you look like you're about to pass out. Come on."

Ignoring her protests, he lifted her easily, taking care not to bump her wounded arm.

"I can walk," she murmured, even as she leaned against the hard wall of his chest.

"Don't argue. Didn't you hear me tell the sheriff I'd take care of you?"

She couldn't tell if he was giving an order or teasing her. And why was she tired again when she felt as if she'd just finished the last nap?

He carried her into her bedroom and placed her on the bed, removing her shoes and tucking her legs beneath the quilt. With economy of motion, he adjusted the pillows beneath her head. Then he eased the ice wrap from around her injured arm and slid a pillow under it, careful not to press on the surgical wound as he arranged it.

"We'll put a fresh one on in about an hour. Let me

get you some water. Those pain pills can dry out your mouth."

"I think I could use a drink."

He was back in seconds with a full glass.

She swallowed some, handed the glass to him, and lay back again, worried about people wasting their time on her when they should be looking for Heather and Trace.

"Don't you have anything better to do than wait on me?" she asked.

His mouth curved in what appeared to be an unfamiliar grin. "Not at the moment. It's my assignment, remember? Now, close your eyes. Maybe you'll catch a little nap."

"If I nap any more today, I won't sleep tonight. I can't believe I'm tired again so soon."

"We'll worry about that tonight. Getting shot takes more out of you than you'd think. The sheriff's wife left some great-looking steaks. I thought I'd grill them tonight and fix potatoes with them."

Her eyes widened. "And a cook, too."

"Just the bachelor basics. And if there's a problem with your arm, I'm happy to cut up your meat."

"Oh, um, thanks. Do you and the sheriff really think whoever shot me will come looking for me again?"

Every trace of humor left his face. "Yes, I do. This wasn't a random thing. The only activity you've been involved in since you got here was looking for your sister and her fiancé, so we can be sure it's connected to that. Which leads me to believe they are still alive and whoever has them is doing their best to make sure we don't find them."

"But, where are they? Who has them? And why? They aren't the kind of people who would hurt anyone."

"That's what we're going to find out. Meanwhile, you take a little nap. I'm leaving the door open in case you need to holler for me."

"God. I hope I can go an hour without bothering you."

"It's no bother," he assured her.

The ache in her arm was beginning to subside, thanks to the pill. Was it also the meds that made her wish the tall, muscular former SEAL was lying in bed next to her? Was she losing her mind?

CHAPTER 9

"Trace?"

Heather pushed closer to Trace, seeking the warmth and assurance of his body.

"Come here."

He wrapped an arm around her shoulders and pulled her more tightly against his body. It was on its way to what people called "full dark," the time of night when Hunter and his partner would be starting the game again. How the fuck did they get themselves into this anyway? Oh, right! They'd been having a snack at the end of a full day of hiking and exploring the area. Trying to decide what to do about dinner. Talking about the huge ranches they'd seen and how great he thought it would be to visit one of them. That he'd always wanted to. Big fucking shot that he was.

He and his big fucking mouth opened the door for the man in the next booth, having coffee with a friend, to introduce himself. Tell him about his big fucking ranch. Offer to give them a tour. Invite them to dinner. Serve them drinks that were obviously drugged.

Obviously because they passed out without even realizing it and woke up in the fucking asshole rough cabin, struggling to stay alive. If they got out of this alive—no, *when* they got out of this alive because he had to believe they would, he was going to spend the rest of his time on Earth making it up to Heather. That is, if she was still speaking to him.

If Heather hadn't started keeping track of the nights they'd been here, he'd have lost count already. Every day and night was the same. Sleep on the pallets on the dirt floor. Eat the cheap food they were being fed. Use the slop buckets. Gather their strength for a night spent eluding capture and injury. Hunted like prey. Avoiding capture and looking for any way possible to escape. Any way they could get over the abominable fencing.

They were filthy dirty and covered with scratches from the wiry bushes they kept brushing against. And tired. So tired. He didn't remember ever being that exhausted. How would they survive even one more night of this dangerous game?

The rumble of a powerful engine grew louder and louder until it stopped right outside the shack. They supposed it to be one of the big four-wheelers that all the ranches seemed to have. That had to mean Hunter came from a distance too great to just walk.

Were they coming from the ranch house? How far away was it?

The wooden door slammed open, startling him. Trace looked up at the hulking figure in the doorway wearing a black shirt and pants with the ever-present hood covering his head. If he weren't so utterly exhausted, Trace would have tried to tackle him, but whoever this was had deliberately kept them weak. Weak enough not to escape but strong enough to continue to play the game.

"Food," the man growled, and set the familiar tray on the floor. "The game starts in one hour." He paused. "Better make it good tonight."

The door closed again, and the rumble growled in the night air.

Heather leaned into Trace, tears leaking from her eyes onto his filthy T-shirt.

"Trace. God, Trace, I don't know if I can do this one more night. We'll just die here."

"I bet you every dollar I'll ever make that your sister is raising hell right now, turning over every rock trying to find us."

"But who's going to listen to her? She doesn't even know anyone out here."

Somehow Trace managed a laugh. "Are you kidding me? Honey, your sister could make the pope sit up and take notice. Let's hang on to that."

Trace had one other thing he kept to himself because he wasn't sure if it would work. As he ran for his life all over these thousands of acres, he'd also continue to look for a chink in the armor—a break in the fence line, any place where they could get through or over. Ever since that first night, he'd been alert for any opportunity at all. Now he was desperate because he knew their time was running out. He had to find the strength for both of them to last a couple more nights. Hunter had said if they did, he'd let them go. Trace didn't believe one word the asshole said, so he needed to have his own escape plan, and he had a couple of possibilities he was going to check again tonight.

"Babe?" He kissed her temple. "I am so sorry I got us into this."

She shifted so she could look at his face.

"Do not say that. I was as tempted and excited to see this place as you were. Neither of us expected we'd land in this kind of hell, but it's as much my fault as yours, so shut up about it, okay?"

"I'm going to find a way out of here before they decide they've had enough fun. I promise you. Meanwhile, we'd better eat, even if it is crap. We need whatever energy we can get."

He dragged the tray over to where Heather sat, stretched out beside her, and uncovered the unappetizing slop. They still needed whatever energy they could get.

They had finished the food and were sitting side by side, holding hands, both of them aware they were approaching the moment Hunter and his friend would decide the game was over and kill them. (And what an appropriate word kill was in this case, Trace thought) when the door slammed open.

It wasn't Hunter but the other man, the one who never spoke to them. Tonight was no different. He pointed to the outside.

Trace stood, holding Heather's hand, and they stumbled out of the crappy shack.

Hunter was waiting, holding his shotgun.

"Time to play." He laughed, a sound more evil than anything Trace ever remembered hearing. "Let's get going."

And so the night began.

∽

HE'D INSISTED she undress before he helped her into bed. The atmosphere between them was so relaxed, she didn't seem the least self-conscious as he helped her remove every item of clothing, even her panties and bra. He eased her under the covers, plumping the pillows beneath her head before he slid in on the other side. He hadn't been with a woman like this for a very long time. His own fault, obsessing with his shortcomings and the evidence of his injuries. His bitterness at his situation didn't help a lot, either. He couldn't believe how lucky he was that Lacey didn't turn away from him.

Now, here they were in her bed and it felt so natural.

"Just keep that arm still," he'd warned her. "You don't want to tear those stitches."

"Uh, okay."

"I mean it. Break the rules and I have to stop whatever I'm doing."

"I'll be good. I promise."

She was so soft, lying next to him, and warm and sweet-smelling. Of course, since the injury, he'd been lucky to be with any woman at all, warm or otherwise. He wasn't sure just how he'd managed this, but he was going to treasure and relish every moment.

He'd made sure when he lay down next to her that he was on the opposite side from her injured arm. Now, he leaned over and placed his mouth on hers, stroking her lips gently with his tongue. Her own small one eased out to touch his before she opened her mouth to welcome him. God, she was so sweet. He slid his tongue over hers, relishing the contact, licking every inch of the inner surfaces.

She started to raise her arm to touch him, but he eased it back down to the bed.

"Uh-uh." He grinned. "I'm doing all the work, remember?"

"That hardly seems fair," she protested. "I get to just lie here and enjoy it."

"Oh, I'm enjoying it, too." His mouth curved into a lazy smile. "More than you know."

He trailed kisses down her neck and over her collarbone, tracing a line with the tip of his tongue as he slid his hand beneath the covers. It made it more tantalizing to explore her this way, even though he'd seen her naked, to reveal her again little by little.

Her breasts were round and plump and fit so nicely in the palm of his hands. He locked his gaze with hers as he brushed his thumb back and forth over a nipple, excited to feel it harden beneath his touch.

He pressed his mouth to hers again as he squeezed the nipple. A tiny sound of pleasure echoed in her throat, so he squeezed again. Then he moved his hand to her other breasts and gave it the same treatment. Finally, he broke the kiss and slid his lips down to take a nipple between his teeth and give it a gentle bite.

"Oh!"

She arched up to him, her little gasp of pleasure sending arrows of heat straight to his begging cock. His very painfully swollen cock.

"Like that, do you?"

"Mmmm."

He almost hummed with satisfaction himself.

"Let's do it again. Okay?"

"Please."

He moved his mouth to the other nipple, sucking hard then closing his teeth gently over it. He teased it, nibbled on it, even as he gently squeezed her breast and kneaded it. The sexy little sounds coming from her mouth sent tingles straight to his balls. Jesus. He was in big trouble here. For a long time, he hadn't had to worry about the niceties of sex, ashamed as he was to admit it. It didn't say much about his attitude or the women he'd chosen to spend time with.

Better take good care of this one, he told himself. Get your shit together.

As she shifted beneath his touch and continued to make those little noises that nearly made his cock explode, he reminded himself this was for her. She deserved every pleasure he could give her.

He leaned his head down and took her mouth again, at the same time sliding his open hand over the curve of her belly, down to that very tempting area between her legs.

"Keep that arm still," he warned as she started to move her injured arm.

"It's hard to keep anything still," she told him, "with you touching me like that."

"Then maybe I ought to stop."

"No!" She practically shouted the words. "I'll keep it still. I promise. Just…don't stop."

He hooked one of his legs over hers, spreading her thighs and opening her up to his touch. He slid two fingers into the wet slit of her sex, seeking her clit and rubbing it over and over. Lacey's moans grew louder, and he could tell she was straining to stay still but fighting a losing battle. When he tugged her clit between two fingers, she tried her best to lift herself to him without moving her arm.

He leaned forward and took her mouth again, this time in a kiss that scorched both of them. He inched her clit between his knuckles, tugging it before finally releasing it but slipping two fingers down and into her hot, wet slit.

"Oh god."

He didn't know how she did it, but she dug her heels into the mattress and lifted her hips without disturbing her injured arm.

"Feel good?" he whispered.

"Better than good. Don't stop. Please."

He moved his fingers faster and faster, adding a third one, filling her completely. He took a nipple into his mouth again, sucking it as he stroked harder and faster, his thumb pressing her clit. Holding her in place with his leg, he rubbed and stroked and rubbed some more until the orgasm finally swept over her. As gently as he could, he held her in place so she wouldn't toss that arm around and rip her stitches, stroking and driving her through her orgasm, thumb pressing down on her clit.

She rode his hand, hard, her slick flesh gripping his fingers as spasm after spasm rocked her, until finally he felt them begin to lessen. At last, he eased his hand from her body, slowly licking each finger as his eyes locked with hers. Her face was flushed, and the pulse at the hollow of her throat beat steadily but much more slowly. He stroked her cheek and lightly touched his mouth to hers.

He was glad he'd been able to give her this pleasure, but of course now his neglected dick was protesting and…

Wolf sat up abruptly in the lounge chair he'd been sprawled in, shocked to discover he was gripping his cock through the fabric of his jeans.

Holy fucking shit!

Was he some horny teenager with no self-control, for god's sake? Had he lost every bit of discipline? What in the ever-lovin' hell was wrong with him? For the first time since what he thought of as "the incident that blew up his life" he'd connected emotionally with a woman, and it apparently was destroying his self-control. The problem was, she was in trouble, wounded, and his protectee. And he'd gone and made a move on her.

Good lord.

What if, for some reason, Alex had shown up again while he was having a teenage sex dream? Or worse yet, Alex's wife? Or Zane? Or any of the other deputies. What the fuck was wrong with him? He swung his legs over the edge of the lounge chair and rose to his feet. In the bathroom, he glanced at the shower, knowing icy streams of water would take care of his problem with his dick, but that would have to wait. He settled for splashing his face and hands with cold water, taking a long moment to be sure he had himself together.

He looked at his watch and saw he'd been asleep for half an hour. He'd decided to take a walk around the property, just to familiarize himself with danger points. Then he studied the house itself, looking for places an intruder could invade. Alex had shown him the security system, which was great, except he knew nothing was failsafe. He hadn't heard a sound from Lacey since he opened his eyes. He just hoped to hell he'd been quiet enough and she hadn't woken up.

The hardest thing was going to be trying to keep his shit together around her, now that his body was broadcasting its reaction to her. Something was brewing between them as it was, even in such a short time, and he didn't want to do something that would turn her away from him. All else aside, they had a crisis about to explode, though, and she was still dealing with her wound. He'd better dig out every bit of that SEAL discipline, take care of the crisis at hand, and then take his cues from her.

Because whatever this thing was—and it shocked him that there was anything at all—it was the first time he'd felt a connection to a human being since the night things literally blew up in his face.

He approached her room quietly. She was lying exactly as he'd left her, and, with her face turned away from him, he tried to tell if she was still asleep. He took a step into the room, cringing when the hardwood floor creaked beneath his foot.

"I hear you." Her voice startled him. "It's okay. I'm not asleep."

"I hope I didn't wake you."

He moved farther into the room, and she turned her head to get a better look at him.

"I wasn't really sleeping. Just lying here, trying not to think. My brain wouldn't shut off."

She tried to push herself to a sitting position but hadn't quite managed to do it one-handed.

"How's the arm?"

"Still hurts but not as much. That ice really helps a lot."

"Let's get you in the other room, and I'll put the ice wrap on again. Here. Let me help you get out of bed."

"Can I just sit here for a second while I get my brain together? I feel as if my world has turned upside down."

"It has, and I have to say you're handling it very well. Here. Let me get you comfortable."

He helped her to sit up and plumped the pillows behind her.

"Thanks." She let out a sigh. "But I'll be very glad when I'm a functioning human being again. This is just crap. My sister's out there somewhere, probably hurt—maybe even dead—and I can hardly even take care of myself."

"That's what you have us for." He sat down next to her, being careful not to jostle her. "Let me tell you about Alex Rossi. He spent eight years as a SEAL, on the toughest assignments. Of course, all SEAL assignments are tough. He didn't re-up because Hank Patterson who owns Brotherhood Protectors convinced him to come here and take this job and clean up a very dirty sheriff's office."

"The rapes." She felt sick.

"Yes. And men who can take care of shit like that can do anything. We'll find them. I promise you."

"But still alive?"

He hated the look of desperation in her eyes. Telling himself to fuck propriety and good sense, he reached for one of her hands and wrapped his around it.

"Yes. Still alive."

Before he could say anything else, his phone buzzed in his pocket. He looked at the readout.

"It's Alex. I'll put it on speaker phone." He punched the button. "Hey, Alex. Lacey and I are together here."

If only.

"I've been talking to Hank Patterson. He's got some ideas he wants to run by us. They've developed a pretty good feel for this area. I've got search and rescue supervising the teams, but Hank and I both think we need a specialized group for this. The more I think about it, the more I get that same feeling running up my spine I got when Micki's dad was killed."

"Good." He looked at Lacey whose face was pinched tight with nerves. "The more the better."

"We'll be there in about an hour. I'm also bringing Zane and another deputy, Jesse Donovan. Another former SEAL. We'll plan this thing like a mission," Alex assured him.

"Good. Excellent. That's exactly what we need."

"The women will be showing up a little later with takeout to feed us. Hope that's okay."

Wolf looked at Lacey, who nodded.

"That's fine," she said into the phone. "And thank everyone."

"It's what we do," Alex told her. "See you when we get there."

Wolf shoved his phone back into his pocket.

"If anyone can find them," he told Lacey, "it's SEALs. And I promise they'll still be alive." He hoped.

"I should get up. I'm sorry, but I think I'll need a little help here."

"Nothing to be sorry for." He squeezed her hand. "Lacey, about earlier today—"

She touched two fingers to his mouth. "If you're going to apologize, I don't want to hear it. I know we've just known each other a couple of days, but intense situations create intense emotions. I'm not sorry I let my guard down a little earlier, and I hope you're not sorry, either."

"But—" How could he explain how conflicted he was? That he wanted her but wanted to protect her and for her not to—

"Whatever is going through that head of yours, get rid of it. Things happen when you least expect it. Let's find Heather and Trace. Then we'll see about everything else." She grabbed his hand. "But, Wolf? I'm not sure I can get through this without you, and I don't mean just as my bodyguard. So, shut up, okay?"

He actually laughed. "Yes, ma'am."

"And now I need to get washed and dressed so I'm presentable for company and can work my brain."

He helped her out of bed, doing his best not to jostle her arm. She managed to brush her hair with one hand, and her teeth. Then he took her back out to the porch and set her up in the lounge chair where, less than an hour ago, he'd stroked himself to an orgasm thinking about her.

Good going, asshole.

But he still wanted her.

First things first.

That meant finding her family and bringing them home safe.

CHAPTER 10

Lacey was sure she'd never been in a room filled with as much testosterone as this one. Wolf had seated her at one end of the dining room table so she wouldn't be next to someone who could jostle her arm. He took the chair to her left, and the others filled the rest of the seats. One thing she was glad of…that all these men were on her side. She was sure they were formidable opponents.

Alex sat at the other end of the table, obviously in charge.

"First, Lacey, as I'm sure Wolf told you. Zane's wife and mine and Jesse's fiancée will be here later. They're bringing dinner, and they wanted the chance to meet you and see if there was anything they could help you with. If you feel up to it, that is."

"I can't—" She stopped. Swallowed. "I can't believe all the kindness. From all of you. I mean, they don't even know me. Why would they go out of their way like this?" She shook her head. Alex grinned. "They're like the Sunshine Club. They all came out of different, desperate situations, especially Zane's wife, and they have become obsessed with the idea of giving back."

"And for god's sake, don't turn them down." Zane gave a fake shudder. "We'll never hear the end of it."

"B-But—" God. She was stammering like an idiot.

"If you aren't ready for the invasion," Alex told her, "please, just say so and I'll head them off."

Lacey wasn't sure what she was, but she did think it might be nice to have some female presence in the mix. She was just such an emotional mess right now, she wasn't sure how to answer him.

"Let me call and head them off." Alex picked up his cell. "You've got enough to deal with."

"No." She shook her head. "Please. I think it's nice they want to do this. If my arm starts to get worse, I'll just get into bed."

"That works. And really, they've all been there one way or another, so they know what the deal is." He looked at Zane. "Especially Lainie."

Lacey thought that must be a hell of a story.

"Okay, then. Lacey, you and Wolf know Zane. This is another one of my deputies, also a former SEAL— Jesse Donovan. And Hank Patterson, head of Brotherhood Protectors, a private security agency based right here. Their offices are in the ranch he owns with his wife, Sadie McClain."

"The actress?" Lacey squeaked the words before

her brain caught up with her. She felt heat creep up her cheeks. "Oh, sorry, but I love her movies."

Hank gave her a tolerant smile. "No problem. She's used to it."

"Except I have family members missing, and the last thing I should be doing is fangirling."

"We'll give you a pass this once." Wolf squeezed her hand. "You need a little something to soften the tension."

Alex cleared his throat. "If I can continue here? Hank's knowledge of the area is second to none. If anyone can figure it out, it's him." He looked over at Wolf. "Plus, he's also a former SEAL."

"Is that a requirement or something?" Lacey blurted the words before she could shut her brain down. God! They'd all think she was a blithering idiot.

But Hank just nodded. "In a way. Just like it is for Alex when he looks for new deputies. Meanwhile, when he called me, I asked him to come out to the house so we could talk and I could use our resources to do some research."

"He has some valuable insights," Alex told them. "His family has lived here for generations, and he's familiar with the people and what goes on around here."

God, Lacey thought. She certainly hoped so.

"Not enough to know the reason the rapes were happening and the circumstances." Hank's words were laced with bitterness.

"I don't think that's something anyone would have just thought about," Jesse told him. "Jesus. Who would?"

"Well, I knew they were being committed once some of the girls were murdered and postmortems showed the evidence. Just not the horrific circumstances."

"Lacey, Alex tells me he's filled you in on the history of that situation."

"He has." She closed her eyes for a moment. "God! What a nightmare."

"It was," Hank agreed. "You should know there are a lot of great people around here, like my family and my in-laws. But there are also those who've grown up through generations of unchallenged privilege. They think laws don't apply to them, and they skirt them all the time."

"And you think one or more of them are somehow involved in Heather and Trace's disappearance?"

Hank nodded. "I do. Maybe they like playing some kind of kidnap scenario. I haven't figured out the details yet, but when Alex and I went over the list of disappearances for the last couple of years, ever since the end of the rapes, at least four of them were in this immediate area. By that, I mean within a ten-mile radius of Eagle Rock."

Lacey was stunned, and she could see that the other deputies were, also.

"And no one thought anything about it?" Zane

asked at last.

Hank shrugged. "Why would they, if they weren't looking for something? Like always, search and rescue scoured the area, as much as they could, but there are so many places to get lost here. We always tell visitors to stick to known paths and stay with civilization. Let me show you the layout."

He'd carried a large document rolled up when he'd walked in. Now he opened it and smoothed it out on the table, using coins to hold down the corners.

"I've been doing a lot of thinking since Alex called me about your sister and her fiancé and about you getting shot. The shooting wasn't a random thing."

"I didn't think so, either," Alex agreed, "but I wanted to run everything past you in case I was looking at this wrong. Thanks for all your insight."

"I want to give you a visual of the area first," he told everyone, looking around the table. "This is a map of where searches are already taking place. We've worked with search and rescue before and refined the map as we did. You can see"—he drew imaginary lines with his finger—"the mountains are almost completely surrounded by private land. The owners prefer to keep travel into the Crazy Mountains at a minimum. There are really only a couple of places you can enter to do any hiking or mountain climbing."

Lacey frowned. "How did that happen? When Heather told me about their trip, she said Trace was really excited because the Crazy Mountains are on public lands, and he had marked out some safe routes."

Hank snorted. "Money. What else. Some of these ranches have been in families for generations. About until about fifty or sixty years ago, no one even questioned it. But then a lot of pressure started to reclaim some of the land for public use. I guess some of the boundaries are not as exact as you'd think. But..." He looked around the table. "As Alex and I discussed, that didn't mean those ranchers rolled over and played dead. This whole area here belongs to four ranches, including Cordell Ritchie's, and they are fierce about ownership. This narrow little road that runs into the Crazies is just outside the whole area."

"So anyone driving to the Crazies has to go this way?" Jesse Donovan asked.

Hank nodded. "Mostly people don't like to use it because they know about the hostilities with the ranchers and prefer a road that leads in from the other side. Anyone taking this road puts themselves at great risk. According to the investigations and the reports from SAR, four of the missing people never found used that particular road."

Jesse frowned. "But why would visitors be in danger? What would someone have to gain? There's no record of anyone being kidnapped and held for ransom. Or any other situation that would cause someone to disappear."

"Unless someone's playing a game." Zane's voice

was icy and expressionless.

"A game?" Lacey's breath caught in her throat. "What game? And what kind of evil people do that?"

The men all exchanged looks.

Wolf took her hand. "My guess is, the same kind who think it's okay fun to rape underage girls."

"On the money," Hank agreed. "It's the only thing we could come up with. Alex agreed, but his version is even worse."

Zane looked at his boss. "What does that mean?"

Alex cleared his throat. "After getting more information on this situation in the past couple of days, I called a friend who's a law officer in Texas. I remembered a story he told me one time about some men in West Texas, big landowners, who got bored and decided to invent a new game. They'd kidnap people late at night from a rest stop, take them to the biggest piece of land, and dump them in an old cabin. They'd feed them enough to keep them alive and then every night they'd let them out and go hunting."

Hank stared at him. "What the fuck?"

"Hunting?" Zane shook his head. "I don't know why anything should shock me anymore, but hunting? People?"

"Yep. They'd tell them if they lasted so many nights, they could go free. Of course they never did. My friend said by the time they'd figured out what the fuck was going on, more than ten people had been killed by these rich assholes who thought it was fun to go hunting people."

Lacey could hardly swallow, her breath trapped in her throat.

"Do you—" She stopped, tried again. "Do you think that's what happened to Heather and Trace?"

"I hope to hell not, but the more I thought about it, the more I couldn't walk away from it. A fair number of people have disappeared in the Crazies, but there was definite evidence most of them had gone exploring into the mountains themselves. You go too deep, you're not careful, anything can happen. There's a fair population of mountain lions and black bear, and they don't like company."

Lacey was doing her best to control the fear that threatened to overtake her.

"Who could be that inhuman?"

"Oh, well." Alex snorted.

"The same kind of people who rape young girls," Hank answered. "I told Alex we need to consider the possibility that some of these rich assholes are involved, just like with the terrible series of rapes. Plus, the way these ranches are protected from public access makes them ideal for something like this. People don't have easy access."

Alex nodded. "How well I know that."

"Cordell Ritchie may try to make himself out as a good citizen," Hank went on, "but he's one of the biggest assholes around. His family's been here for generations, he's got more money than you can count, and he and his asshole buddy Frank Weathers are always looking for the next thrill. The next challenge. Hell, they bet ten thousand dollars on what the temperature would be like the next day. I was shocked when I didn't snag them in the rape situation, but there was no evidence pointing to them, and no one wanted to talk about them."

"Apparently," Alex added, "they think the rules don't apply to them."

"But he offered to help with the search and rescue effort," Lacey reminded them. "Told me how sorry he was my family had gotten lost."

"He knows how to play people," Hank said. "Always has. My dad never had a good thing to say about him."

"And," Wolf added, "I'll bet the reason he wants to be so neighborly and help with the search is so he can steer it away from wherever he's got people holed up."

Jesse leaned forward. "Only we aren't going to let that happen. You can bet on it."

"So, what do we do?" she asked, looking from Alex to Hank to Wolf. Fear had her gripped so tightly, she could barely breathe.

"We mark out the area we're going to search, and when it's dark, we make our move."

"But won't they be expecting you?"

Alex shook his head. "I already sent the sections I marked as primary to the head of search and rescue. Ritchie is probably going to say he'll search his geographic area, but we're going to tell him we don't believe our targets even went there. Rob

Harrison from SAR can handle that message very well."

"Does Rob know what you suspect?" Wolf asked.

"He does. He's trustworthy and one of the smartest men I know. He also thinks Ritchie is a dangerous problem and agrees with my assessment. The guy is an egomaniac who's gotten away with things all his life. Rob will handle it on his end. He's going to call all the people who volunteered to become team leaders and get them going right away."

"But it will be dark soon," Lacey protested. "And aren't you afraid if he does have them, he'll panic and just kill them and bury their bodies?"

It was Hank who answered her. "No. His ego's too big for that. He's smart enough to shut down his game for tonight and then plan for the big finale tomorrow night. We'll be ready for him. We want to catch him in the act. If we keep Ritchie occupied tonight—and he's already volunteered—then tomorrow night he'll make his move, and we'll catch him and find Heather and Trace."

"But—"

"Lacey." Wolf squeezed the hand he'd continued holding all this time. "Look at it this way. Alex and Hank have been doing the things they do for a very long time. If they thought playing it this way was too dangerous, they'd head out there right now. But they don't want Ritchie to panic and decide to kill them tonight to be safe. I'm sure there's a secure gate with a call box, and enough time that if Alex announces himself, Ritchie can refuse him entrance and get his ass out to dispose of Heather and Trace."

"If we get him off his guard," Alex added, "he's arrogant enough to want one more night of his game before he gets rid of them. But it won't be tonight because he's leading an SAR team tonight. We hunt as long as people can keep going, and it's actually easier to locate things when it's dark. We have SAR dogs, and the scent stabilizes the later it gets. And if we want to put on a good show for him, we need to follow our usual procedure. Not make him think we suspect anything."

"If Alex and Hank thought they should move tonight, they wouldn't be sitting here now," Wolf assured her. "But remember, there's always the chance we're wrong and they're someplace else, so we don't want to overlook anything. I promise you."

"Okay." But everything inside her was screaming to go now and get this done.

"Lacey?" She looked over at Jesse, who hadn't said much. "When we planned rescue missions as SEALS, our first reaction was always to gear up and get going, but a good rescue mission takes planning if you want to keep the hostages safe. I know it's hard, but I'm asking you to trust us on this."

She looked around the table at each of the men. On every face, she saw the same thing: determination to successfully execute without harm to the hostages. And Jesse was right. They all had years of experience at this. She had to put her faith in that.

"I believe you. I do."

"And they won't want to rush it," Wolf added. "In fact, I suspect there might be a few extra things planned for the big finale tomorrow night."

Jesse cleared his throat. "And if we keep Ritchie occupied tonight, that gives us extra time to prepare. I want this done right. I don't think he and whoever he's playing this game with will go hunting tonight. They'll be out putting on a good show as concerned citizens, leading a search party someplace that is not his ranch. I promise you."

"Plus," Alex added, "I want to get a plat of his land from the county assessor's office and see if there's a shack on their property and where it's located. I want to do this right. If we lull him into false security, our chances are better of no one getting hurt."

"Like I said, I believe in you guys. Heather is all the family I have left, so I'm sure you know where my head and heart are, but I believe you can pull this off. I just have one more question."

"Let's have it," Alex told her.

"I'm guessing when he approached me at the gas station, he knew who I was because I haven't exactly made myself invisible. But he wasn't really offering to help, was he?"

"No." Hank was the one who answered her. "I'm sorry, but he was trying to insert himself into the situation so he could find out what's going on."

She sighed. "I should have had a better read on him."

Wolf squeezed her hand. "Don't beat yourself up over it. There is absolutely no way you could have known that."

"Okay, people." Alex looked at the map. "Let's make some plans here."

As Lacey listened to them, she realized that if she could depend on anyone to know what they had to do and do it successfully, it was a group of SEALs, particularly these SEALs. She was stunned at the plan of action Alex and Hank brought to the table, and at the input from the others. Despite her worries and fears, she actually had a sense this rescue would succeed.

"One more thing," Alex told her as he rolled up the map. "Hank and I are convinced Ritchie is the one who shot you. He has a reputation for being a crack shot with his rifle. I got the slug they took out of your arm from the doc at the hospital. If and when it turns out to be Ritchie, I have something for comparison."

"Do you think he'll try again?"

"I'd like to say no, but with him, who knows? He might be feeling overconfident and think he can find a place to take a shot. If he does, it will be tonight when he thinks no one has eyes on him and he's not doing whatever it is with his captives."

"I just can't imagine why he would have kidnapped them. They certainly wouldn't have been sticking their nose in his business."

"You never know what they might have stumbled

over by accident. I don't trust a thing that man does. Wolf has his handgun and his rifle, and he's a crack shot, so you'll be well protected."

Lacey suddenly realized she heard car doors slamming in the driveway then the doorbell rang.

"Someone's here."

Alex smiled at her.

"I'll get it. The ladies have arrived with dinner. Stay right here. I'll bring them in to meet you. Jesse and Zane, you guys help with the food, okay?"

"Got it."

Lacey sat there, both eager and apprehensive, Wolf holding her hand until Alex returned with three women. They were all dressed casually in jeans and shirts. One of them, a fairly tall woman in jeans and a T-shirt, with thick brown hair pulled back in a clip, came right up to her and gave her a wide smile.

"Hi. I'm Micki Rossi. Don't get up, please. I'm sure getting shot is a very unpleasant experience. I just wanted to meet you, make sure you found everything here okay, and give you my number in case you need something." She took Lacey's free hand and gave it a soft squeeze.

So this was the very rich high-powered prosecuting attorney who had made everything so comfortable for them? Lacey wasn't sure what she'd expected, but Alex Rossi's wife came across more like the woman next door, which relieved her.

"Oh. Everything's great. Thank you so much for arranging all this. I'm—overwhelmed."

Micki laughed. "Consider it bribery. Alex wants to make sure Wolf takes the job, so it's important you two feel welcome."

"Oh." Lacey was startled. "But I'm not with—We're not—I'm just—"

"Uh-huh." Micki grinned and glanced at Lacey's handheld firmly by Wolf. "Let me introduce the others."

Lainie Halstead was shorter than Micki, with delicate features, rich auburn hair, and a warm smile.

"Welcome." She held her hand out to Lacey, who couldn't help noticing the shadows that still drifted in the woman's eyes.

"Thank you."

The last one to greet her was Terry Fordice, medium height, with nice curves, and coffee-colored hair. Lacey knew she was engaged to Jesse, and they were planning to get married in a couple of months.

"How are you feeling?" Terry asked her. "I can't believe that bastard shot you. I'd like to take a rifle to his balls."

The other women grinned, and Lacey just stared. Terry did not at all look like someone who would be spitting out expressions like that.

"Terry's an Alcohol, Tobacco, and Firearms agent," Micki explained. "Works out of the field office in Billings. She's our resident tough cookie. Don't let us scare you off, Lacey. We're really nice, gentle people."

At that, all three of them burst out laughing.

"Okay, enough with teasing our guest." Alex kissed his wife on the cheek. "We need to eat and get moving. What did you guys bring to feed us?"

"Barbecue from The Hitching Post," Micki told him. "I didn't think anyone wanted to clean up the mess from cooking. We'll have it on the table in a few minutes. There's cold beer in the fridge, and I just brought some wine. Lacey, would you like to have a glass? I have white and red."

"I'd love one." And wasn't that an understatement. "It's been long enough since I took the last pain pill that I think it's okay. And white, please."

Yes, she definitely needed something to soothe her nerves.

"Food's ready," Micki told her when she delivered the wine. "Alex, I assume you're going to swallow it whole and get going?"

He gave her a quick kiss. "You know me so well. But we can't waste any time. Like I said earlier, if we haul ass out there tonight, I'm afraid if this is a kidnap situation of some kind, for whatever reason, the person responsible will panic and get rid of them before we find them. Plus, the other teams are already out on their routes. I want to get reports on where they are and also where Cordell Ritchie has taken his team."

"You really think he's involved?" Lacey asked.

"My gut tells me he is, and that gut has saved my life more than once. But if he's using them for a twisted game, we have to be extra careful how we do this. I want to see if I can figure it out before we go barging onto his ranch. If that's where he has them, I'm sure he's got someone he trusts a lot to get rid of them immediately and I want to avoid that."

"Yes, please."

"Then, Wolf, I think we're going to ride the perimeter in a four-wheeler I've got stashed in the barn. I want to make sure no one's lurking in the shadows or hiding in the trees, and show you the areas to keep a lookout for."

Wolf frowned. "Shouldn't one of us stay with the women, just as a matter of course?"

"Terri, you're hanging around?" Alex asked.

"I said I was. Right?" She turned her back to him and lifted the hem of her shirt to reveal a handgun in a holster tucked in the small of her back. "We're good."

"Sorry. Just double-checking. My gut tells me we've got a volatile situation here."

Lacey knew he wanted the woman there because she was armed. Good, not that she wanted these people—whoever they were—to come storming the house. Lacey had the weird feeling she might have fallen into a television show or a movie, but as she looked at everyone standing in the room, for the first time since she'd boarded the plane to Montana, she had a hopeful feeling.

"I'm not sure how to thank all of you."

"No thanks necessary," Micki told her. "It's what we do. What we've *learned* to do."

Wolf rejoined them as soon as he'd put food out for Bailey.

Lacey had wondered how they'd actually sit through a leisurely meal under the circumstances, but there was nothing leisurely about the way the men ate. They scarfed their food and were heading toward the side door while still chewing.

"I'm leaving Bailey here, too," Wolf told her. "He can't shoot a gun, but he could practically take a guy's leg off with his teeth."

Lacey grinned. "That's very comforting."

As if he understood what Wolf was saying, Bailey came and sat down beside her, as he'd done a few times earlier, every bit of him totally alert.

"You've got quite the protector there," Lainie observed.

"And we've just met." Lacey grinned and took another sip of wine.

"Would you be more comfortable in bed?" Micki asked.

"No." Lacey shook her head. "If I need to get there, I'll let you know. I'm really interested in how you hooked up with all these guys. It'll keep my mind off what's happening and from trying to figure out who shot me and what I did to make it happen."

"Okay, then. Let's get a refill on the wine."

CHAPTER 11

The four-wheeler in the barn was rigged to carry four people. Hank Patterson had to leave, so the others climbed on with Alex in the driver's seat. The properties on either side of this one were as large or larger. One had a good-sized corral in the backyard.

"The Fallons have two horses," Alex explained. "They let them outside a lot so they get plenty of air and sunshine."

"Nobody out here is fenced," Wolf commented, as they rode the length of the property.

"Not much need for it," Zane told him. "For the most part, things are fairly quiet around here."

"Well, with a few exceptions," Jesse reminded him.

"Okay, I want to check these stands of sycamores and quaking aspens out there. They're toward the back of the property and grow tall and thick. Just like the trees by the road where Lacey was shot," he reminded Wolf. "But sneaking onto any of the properties right around here is very chancy. People protect their land. They shoot first and ask questions later. Oh, some brave, adventurous soul could try to sneak onto one of your neighbors' properties and get to your place that way, but their chances of success are severely limited."

"And of course," Wolf reminded him, "I have Bailey. He may not be fit for military duty any longer, but, for our purposes, he's rock solid."

"Good to know."

"I'm not too sure whoever this is would try another hit," Jesse said. "Not with Lacey now being the center of attention. But then, if whoever has kidnapped her relatives is one of the men raping young girls, who just never was caught, well, that kind of person has balls of steel and an ego bigger than Montana. They think they're invincible."

"You've got that right," Zane agreed. "Those kinds of men think they're invincible. The man Lainie was with in Tampa was an out and out abuser, powerful, rich, who thought he could get away with anything. Even tracked her here to Eagle Rock and tried to kill her."

"What happened?" Wolf asked.

"I killed the fucker," Zane told him. "Drilled a hole in his forehead. Just like we'll do with anyone who tries to harm Lacey."

Wolf was suddenly filled with a surge of emotion he hadn't felt in a long time. What if he had just kept ignoring Zane Halstead's calls? What if he hadn't gotten his shit together and decided to see if this was actually a restart on his life? He didn't even want to think about it. He made a silent vow to do whatever it took to keep Lacey safe and help bring her family back safe.

And figure out what to do about his feelings for her that hit him like a giant thunderbolt and caught him totally off guard.

"Well, you've got a good visual of the property," Alex told him as he pulled the four-wheeler into the barn. "Here's the keys to this beast in case you need it. Don't hesitate to take it out to patrol the property now and then. Just the sight of it might discourage anyone who wants to take a shot at Lacey."

"Thanks." He shoved the key ring into his pocket. "Sounds like a good idea, although I hope your plan works and tomorrow night you wrap this up."

"You know, it could have been one of the other assholes around here who thinks he's bigger than god and has the money to prove it, but my bet is on Ritchie. When I was in the SEALs, my Team leader used to say I could sniff out the bad guys buried in a crowd. I hope that sense is still working. I was surprised we didn't scoop him up with the other vermin raping girls, but he somehow managed to evade being caught with the others. Not enough pointed in his direction, and no one gave him up."

"I guess there is such a thing as loyalty among snakes." Disgust dripped from Zane's voice.

Just as they reached the house, Alex's phone rang. He looked at the screen.

"It's Jules. She volunteered to stay late tonight and coordinate the search. Hold on."

He walked away as he answered the call.

"Jules Ravenal is Alex's office manager," Zane told him. "The one who worked under the previous sheriff who retired in the midst of all the dirt going on. Jules was so grateful her old boss was in jail and Alex was cleaning things up, she pleaded her case with him so he'd keep her. It's worked out great. She's terrific."

"Okay." Alex was shoving the phone back in his pocket as he walked back to them. "Gotta go, guys. Jules has the big board set up in the office, and the teams are calling in with whatever they find…or don't find, as it seems is the case. We need to take a look at it and also reassign our own patrols for tonight. Wolf, I—"

Wolf held up his hand. "I'm good. Go do what you have to do. That's the priority right now."

Everyone shook hands and then they were gone.

When Wolf entered the house, the women were just cleaning up the last remnants of dinner. Lacey had moved into the kitchen to chat with them while they worked.

"And we're done." Micki Russo turned to Lacey and smiled. "We're going to leave you and Wolf alone. I think you guys are all set now, right?"

Wolf nodded. "Lacey, you need anything?"

"Only to thank these wonderful women for making me feel so welcome and taking care of everything."

Lainie took her hand. "We all know what it's like to be in a bad situation, but I'm telling you, you're at the right place for help. These guys will bring Heather and Trace home safe and sound, and then we'll all celebrate."

"Maybe we'll even convince you to stick around for a while," Micki teased.

"We'll see."

The weird thing was, she hadn't been in the area for more than two weeks, yet she felt strangely at home, more than she did in Nevada. And she recalled again how she and Heather and Trace had talked about exploring the area and thinking about relocating. As a freelance wildlife photographer, Heather could work from anywhere, plus Montana was loaded with opportunities for photographs. She could pitch it to any number of publications. Even do a coffee table book.

But right now, all she wanted was to see them alive and healthy and happy right in front of her. That came first.

"You look a little worn out."

"Oh!" She hadn't heard Wolf come back into the house, and his voice startled her.

"Sorry." He looked down at her and grinned. "I'll make more noise the next time."

"Don't worry. I think I'm just jumpy."

"And with good reason. Listen, I'm going to take Bailey out back for a few, give him some exercise and stuff. I know you've been exhausted today. I mean, one day after surgery and all, and it's been a challenging day. Want me to help you into bed? I mean, uh…"

She chuckled. "I know what you mean. I am tired, but it was nice on the porch before. I think I'd like to sit out there and watch you and Bailey, if that's okay."

Bailey, who again had been sitting beside her, perked up his ears and gave a gentle *ruff*.

"I think he's talking to you," Wolf teased. "He's saying yes."

"Then that settles it. And you don't have to carry me. I can walk. It was only my arm, for heaven's sake."

"You had surgery, Lacey. Big or small, it's an assault on your body. Plus, you had a general anesthetic. Give yourself a break. And I'd bet money you haven't slept much since you got here."

She sighed. "No bet there. I think I'll forgo another pain pill if I can have one more glass of wine. Then I'll be ready for bed."

"Coming right up," he told her.

He got her situated on the porch with her wine. Then he took Bailey out into the yard, although as big as the area was, a yard didn't seem a large enough description. As he stood outside in the fading sunlight, tossing a stick for the dog and playing games with him, Lacey sitting on the porch sipping her wine, he thought how easy it would be to get used to this. Alex Russo had turned out to be a dream of a leader, and the deputies were great guys that he related to. Maybe because they were all former SEALs, but still.

He hoped they found Lacey's family soon and that he could persuade her to stick around for a while afterward. Maybe see where things could go between them.

After two days? Am I crazy?

Maybe, but it never hurt to ask.

CORDELL RITCHIE STOPPED on the trail he was walking, pissed beyond belief. Why the fuck weren't things working out for him the way they were supposed to? He'd been damn lucky when Alex Rossi, charging in on his white horse, had totally missed him on the sweep rounding up the others who were stupid and got caught. But the others had made several mistakes when they had their fun with the young girls. Someone spotted them. The girls talked, especially after the fucking sheriff got sent off to prison for getting rid of the "evidence."

A very tiny few of them escaped undetected. However, the game was over. They'd had to take their sexual escapades into the city and find women who were over eighteen to fulfill their perverted desires. But that didn't satisfy them. Ritchie, along with his asshole buddy Bryson Hall, had to find something else.

That's when The Hunt was born.

They were sitting around drinking hundred-dollar-a-bottle bourbon in his den one night, their wives off on a spa weekend, and half watching a movie about big game hunting. And that's when the idea came to them. Oh, they hunted elk every year in the Crazies, but the challenge was fading.

What if they hunted humans? Turned part of one of their ranches into a human game preserve. See how long it took to wear them down. They'd set a time limit. If their prey survived, then they'd let them go. Of course, they only hunted at night, and so far, no one had survived. Not that they intended them to. One corner of Cordell's ranch had turned into a graveyard, with the bodies buried deep.

They had to choose carefully. People who could be trapped without anyone noticing. People who were alone or with just one other person. People without ties in the area, who wouldn't be missed for a while. Folks disappeared in the Crazies often enough that it didn't set off any alarm bells. When family or friends came looking for them, well, there were plenty of stories about strangers disappearing in the Crazies to make it believable.

This couple, Heather and Trace, were the best so far. Smart, inventive, strong, and supporting each other. They'd survived longer than anyone else. It was almost a shame to kill them. They'd never find anyone else quite as challenging.

But that fucking Cooper woman had blown it all up. Destroyed a good thing. Too bad his shot didn't get her that day on the road. And who the fucking hell figured she'd been on her way to see that shithead Rossi, the sheriff who spoiled everyone's fun? He'd just tracked her since that day at the truck stop and figured that two-lane highway was a good place to do the job.

Shit, shit, shit.

Thank the lord Rossi had agreed to let him lead one of the search and rescue teams. He'd keep them far away from his own place, that was for damn sure. And he'd make sure Bryson did, too. Oh, yeah, the association had been only too glad to jump in and lend a hand, under his guidance. The smartest thing he'd done was to volunteer.

He'd give the couple a reprieve for one night while he worked the search. Only, at some point he'd find an excuse to break away. He'd discovered where Lacey Cooper was being housed, and he planned on finishing what he'd started with her. Even if she had one of those damn SEALs as a bodyguard. He'd take him out, too.

But it all had to be done carefully, and he couldn't get caught. Not if he wanted his grand finale tomorrow night. Then he and Bryson would have to cool it for a while, but that was okay. There was always some other game they could devise to entertain themselves.

He looked at his watch. Nine fifteen. He'd stay with this team he was leading for another hour before making some kind of excuse to get away. He wanted to stop by his captives and bring them food so they wouldn't starve to death first. He'd tell them they were getting a little reprieve tonight. Maybe fool them into thinking he might have decided just to let them go. Then, tomorrow night, when the first intensity of the search had waned, he could have an exciting finish to the game. Maybe their hope would give them extra energy, and the final hunt would be even more exciting.

Just thinking about it made his dick harden.

And that was another plus to this little game. With access to young girls in the area cut off when the new sheriff arrived, his sex life had dwindled to almost nothing. After thirty years of marriage and his wife's lack of interest in anything a little different, he'd been forced to take himself in hand if he wanted satisfaction.

Until The Hunt.

After that first time, he'd discovered with a shock how sexually gratifying it could be. What would he do when they had to shut things down?

Oh, well, a question for another day. Right now, he had business to take care of. And that included checking on that bitch Lacey Cooper. He needed to make sure she was still in the same place and not running around causing more trouble, although getting Rossi to do this all-out search was certainly bad enough.

If only he hadn't missed her when he shot at her. He was a crack shot, and he aimed right at the side of her head. But the damn horse had shifted just enough to throw his aim off.

He didn't know if she'd mentioned to the sheriff or whoever that he'd spoken to her at the truck stop, but hell. He was just being a concerned citizen. No one could read anything into that, right? And he had no idea why he felt the need to check on her, but he knew he'd sleep better if he did.

Damn it to hell anyway. How had things gotten so unbelievably fucked up?

∽

HEATHER LEANED against Trace's body, grateful for the security of his arm around her. No one had brought them food tonight, even though it had been dark for quite a while and hunger pains stabbed at her stomach. Not that they'd been given a whole lot of food to begin with, just enough to keep them alive, but their bodies were used to it.

"Maybe they decided to starve us to death," she murmured, pressing harder against Trace's side.

"It's a thought," he agreed, "but I don't think so. They like The Hunt too much. Something's happened to interfere with the schedule."

Heather turned her head to look at him. "I just know my sister's out there making a lot of noise. Lacey's really good about banging on people's doors and stirring up action. We just have to hang on long enough until she gets a good search party going."

Trace shrugged. "Anything is possible. It's been almost a week since she heard from us. How long would she wait before making a big fuss?"

Heather managed a little laugh. "If she waited more than two days to get something going, I'd be shocked."

"So maybe she's here and stirring the pot and that's why the routine has changed."

"Oh my god. If only. Except…no one even knows us around here, and I heard people go camping all over the Crazies and disappear all the time. What if we just get written off? I mean, there must be a search and rescue organization, but without a clue as to where we might be…"

"Lacey will figure out something," Trace assured her. "Your sister is like a dog with a bone. And thank god for that."

"I hope she makes it soon. I'm not sure how much longer I can hold out. God! My legs are a mess from those bushes, and I've got bruises everywhere from bumping into trees. And I'm so tired I can hardly move, much less get away from these maniacs with rifles." Tears leaked from the corners of her eyes. "Last night, I wondered if it might not be better to just let them shoot me and get it over with."

Trace cupped her chin and turned her to face him, kissing the tears that tracked down her cheeks.

"That would definitely not be better. What would I do without you? I told you, I think I found a way out of here. I was planning to check it tonight to make sure. Because I promise you, we will get out of here." He brushed a kiss over her dried and cracked lips. "This is my fault. I was such a jackass wanting to see a "real" ranch. I'm going to spend the rest of our lives making it up to you."

"You had no way to predict something like this would happen. That man seemed so nice when he was talking to us."

"Yeah, some people are really good at playing roles, especially when they want something."

At that moment, they heard the bar outside the door being moved, and the door swung inward. Hunter strode into the shack, carrying the familiar tray. He set it down near their feet.

"This is your lucky night, you two."

"Are—Are you letting us go now?"

To Heather, the laugh sounded like pure evil.

"Not tonight. I unfortunately have something to do that prevents the evening's entertainment. But if you are very, very good, tomorrow night might be your last here. You've earned the right to end this game."

Heather hated the little feeling of hope that jumped in her chest.

"So we can go after that?" Trace asked. "You'll

keep your word? That if you hadn't caught us by the end of the game, we were free? And when does the game end? You never told us? When do we earn our freedom?"

"I always keep my word. You've been very good at this, so I'd say we're getting close to the end of the game. Now, you'd better eat your dinner to keep up your strength."

Then he was gone.

Silence shimmered for a long moment.

"Do you think he means it?" Heather finally asked.

"Maybe. The question is how he means it? Does he plan to actually let us go or does he plan to kill us tomorrow night? Is that what he means when he says tomorrow night could be our last one here?"

"I don't trust one word he says. You know the goal of the game is to kill us. But hang on, sweetheart. Whatever I need to do, tomorrow night I'm getting us out of here. All we need is to get out of this cabin." He hugged her against him. "And trust me, babe, when we do, I mean what I say."

"Okay."

Or die trying.

~

HE WAS VERY careful approaching the area where the house was that Lacey Cooper was staying in. It had been a damn good piece of luck that he'd discovered it, although he realized he couldn't take another shot at her here. If only the one he'd taken when she was driving on that two-lane highway had hit something vital. Too bad, although shots like that were always chancy. And here they'd have at least one person guarding her. He'd dismissed killing the guard after he'd learned the place had a top-notch alarm system. He'd never get close enough. Paying people to keep you informed was a damn good investment.

Although, what the hell good it would do him to lay eyes on her, he had no idea. And he hated to admit that killing the guard would accomplish nothing.

Leave it alone. Go home.

He should have stayed with the team he was leading, but he was too on edge.

He happened to know that the owners of the property backing up to where the Cooper woman was were out of town. Their driveway wasn't visible from where she was, so he could park there and hike until he had a good view. It didn't have to be too far. He had expensive high-power binoculars. On the other hand, maybe they had someone out patrolling the area looking for just this thing.

He was still silently debating with himself when he reached his destination. There was zero traffic on the little two-lane country road, so he traveled the last quarter mile without lights. He parked in the driveway in front of the garage so his car would be hidden. Then, dressed in all black, he began his hike across the property until he was close enough to get a good look.

The lights were on in the house he was heading toward but only in a couple of rooms. He wondered how many people were guarding her? When he reached a thick stand of trees, he stopped, leaned against a broad trunk, and took out the binoculars.

The house inside looked empty, but he knew that was not the case. His source told him there was definitely a guard there, some new guy the sheriff was hiring. Ritchie studied every room he could see but they all seemed empty. So, where the fuck was everyone?

A few minutes went by and then he saw someone move into the kitchen where a night-light over the stove was on. Wow. Whoever this was, he was sure as hell big. And he walked with the lithe grace of an athlete. Or the military, Ritchie thought. Maybe he's another of those former SEALs Rossi is hiring. Not good. Those guys didn't take shit from anyone.

The man left the kitchen and then his shadow moved across the curtains in a room at the end of the house. Bedroom, he thought. Where the bitch is sleeping. Not that it mattered. He wasn't getting close, but at least he was satisfied she was tucked away here. Maybe if it took long enough for her to recover from the gunshot, the search would end without results, and she'd go home.

Maybe.

Just then the door to the porch opened, and the

man stepped out with... Wait! Was that a dog? And a damn big one at that. The man put his hand on the dog's head, probably to control him. Thank god he wasn't letting him race across toward where Ritchie was hiding. He'd be in deep shit.

Ritchie had to shift position a little what with trees here and there blocking his line of sight. Of course, it also meant the man couldn't see him, either. Did he sense something? He needed to get the hell out of there before the guy decided to take a look around.

Tomorrow, after the last night of The Hunt, he'd figure out how to get rid of the woman, and the man, too, if he had to. There'd be no one left to go looking or raise a stink. And trying to find missing people in the Crazies was impossible. But they already knew that, right?

CHAPTER 12

FALLING asleep was harder than Lacey expected. She managed to get into bed without too much help from Wolf. Taking off her clothes was a challenge and, to Wolf's credit, he did his best to avert his eyes when he could. But the range of motion of her injured arm prevented her from doing a lot of things by herself. At least she had privacy in the bathroom, thank god.

She was exhausted by the time she'd brushed her teeth and managed to get into a nightgown. Wolf had turned back the covers like a servant waiting on the lady of the house and adjusted her in bed the way he had for her nap. She'd had ice on her arm during the evening, so she insisted she didn't need any when she got into bed.

Bailey, who seemed to have adopted her, sat beside her bed while Wolf fetched a glass of water from the kitchen and set it on her nightstand.

"I'm setting your meds here, too. You won't need the antibiotic again until morning but you might need a pain pill tonight."

"Let's hope I don't." They might dull the pain, but they also dulled everything else. She didn't like the feeling at all.

"I get it, but I'm telling you, don't think you're being brave. I tried that and, let me tell you, it sucked."

"Except I promise you your injury is much worse than mine."

She'd noticed him now and then favoring his shoulder, like when he was trying to be heroic and carrying her to her bedroom.

"I'm good. Listen, do you want the light on? Off? If you're set, I'm going to check the back for a minute. Something is making the back of my neck itch. I don't think there's anyone out there. And even if there is, they can't get close enough without setting off an alarm."

"I'm good. But…would you come back and talk to me for a while after?"

She felt stupid for asking him, like a kid who was afraid of the dark, but he just nodded.

"No problem. Be right back. Come on, Bailey."

She had to smile when Bailey just sat there, looking from one to the other.

"Go on, Bailey," she told him. "I'll be okay till you get back."

"You have no idea," Wolf told her, "how rare it is for that to happen. Especially since he and I had established our bond long before this."

"I don't want to upset you," she told him and was relieved when he smiled.

"Not happening. I'm just glad to see he has such good taste. I'll be right back."

"Go on, Bailey," she told him.

Bailey still sat for a moment, but then a tiny growl rumbled up from his throat.

"He senses something," Wolf explained. "Come on, Bailey, let's see what's got you hot and bothered."

Lacey had heard it was exceedingly rare for dogs trained like Bailey to split their affections. Maybe it was a sign of something, but what? Wolf had been the one to find her on the side of the road and the one assigned to guard her. Maybe the universe was trying to send her a message.

But first, before anything else, she had to find Heather and Trace. With each passing day and now every passing hour, she was feeling more and more depressed. Alex Rossi had teams of people out looking everywhere for them, people who knew the mountains and the area and who had committed to not giving up until they found her family.

"Well, something disturbed him." Wolf walked back into the room, Bailey at his side. He was holding the laptop. "I have no idea what it was. Nothing was moving out there. I waited a while then Bailey seemed to relax a little. Whatever it was apparently moved on."

"Do you think someone was spying on us?" *Oh god!*

"Hard to say. If they were, they're gone. I checked the camera feeds and didn't see anything, but I'm keeping this next to me." His face was set in a hard line. "Don't' worry, Lacey. Nobody's getting past me to you."

"I don't even understand what they want?" she cried. "I mean, if someone really has Heather and Trace, I have no idea what for. And why are they after me after I've already talked to Alex and set this whole thing in motion."

"We aren't sure anyone has them," he reminded her. "It's just the strongest of Alex's theories and, if so, the reason isn't obvious. Maybe they just want to retaliate for you igniting this massive search and rescue operation. But I promise you, we're going to find them. and nothing is going to happen to you."

"But how, if you don't know who they are, or even if there is a they?"

"There's no other reason someone would take a shot at you," Wolf pointed out. "You must have been rattling cages louder than they wanted."

"And they thought killing me would solve their problem?"

"Look at it this way. No one else had given you much more than lip service. Even SAR had called it quits after a day. Rossi is still an unknown quantity to a lot of people. They might have figured if they got you before you talked to him, the whole search thing would die down. And even if he investigated your murder, there are no clues. No place to look, no place to go."

"I've just had this feeling from the beginning they're in terrible danger."

"And that's why Alex jumped in the way he did. Now. As they kept telling me when I was in the hospital, you'll heal faster if you let yourself sleep."

"I'm sure you paid a lot of attention to them," she teased.

He laughed, a strangely rusty sound. "Yeah, well, at least try to rest."

She wet her lips. "Could I ask you a favor?"

"Sure. Whatever you need."

"Could you… Would you…just stay in here with me a while?" She held her breath, wondering if she'd pushed too hard.

He only hesitated a moment. "Sure. No problem. Let me see if there's a comfortable chair out here I can drag in."

"Wait." She swallowed, not meaning to say the word so loud. "I mean, please wait. You don't need to stress your shoulder dragging furniture around." She bit her lower lip. "You, um, could lie down next to me. Here. On top of the covers, of course."

She watched a smile tease at his lips. "You sure it's okay?"

"If you don't mind. I'd, uh, feel safer."

They stared at each other for a long moment. Lacey wondered if she was the only one who felt all that electricity arcing between them. Maybe she was making a mistake here but, for some reason, she just needed reassurance of his presence.

He stared down at her for a long moment before he finally nodded. "Okay. I guess. But you get Bailey, too. We're a package deal."

"I wouldn't have it any other way."

"Let me do one more turn around the house, and we'll settle down for the night."

While they did their last look-see, Lacey asked herself at least a hundred times if she was doing something stupid. She was a grown woman. She didn't need someone to hold her hand. She was well protected without Wolf being in the room with her. Still…

"All set." His voice jarred her out of her thoughts.

"Okay, then. Good."

"Slide over," he told her. "I'd feel better between you and the door."

"Really?" She frowned. "You think someone would actually come into the house?"

"Just doing things the way I was trained."

Before she knew what he was doing, he picked her up gently and slid her over to the other side of the bed, without even jostling her arm. Next, he pulled his gun from where he'd stashed it at the small of his back and placed it on the nightstand. Finally, he toed off his boots and eased himself down beside her.

"Be careful of your shoulder," she cautioned.

"I'm good. Close your eyes and try and get some sleep."

"Thanks," she told him. "For doing this."

"No problem. Pleasant dreams."

She fell asleep imaging a naked Wolf in bed with her, his mouth everywhere on her body.

~

Wolf's phone on the nightstand woke him with its insistent ring tone. He blinked his eyes, disoriented for a moment at where he was. In bed. With Lacey Cooper.

What the hell!

Then he remembered her plea the night before and his need to make her feel more secure.

Be honest, jerko. You like being needed again, Contributing something useful.

And lying here next to a beautiful woman who has made responses that have been dead for a long time come roaring to life.

The phone sounded again and, when he picked it up, he saw Alex's number on the screen.

"What's up?"

"Hope I didn't wake you." Alex's voice sounded like he hadn't had much sleep the night before.

"No, I'm good. What's going on?"

"We had a lot of teams out last night covering this entire county and parts of the two adjoining ones."

Wolf sat up and swung his legs over the side of the bed, taking care not to jostle Lacey.

"And?"

"And, on the one hand, no one found a trace of them. But on the other hand, I'm not the only one who thinks Cordell Ritchie might be involved."

Now Wolf really was on the alert. "What happened?"

"One of the people on his team called to tell me the guy was acting weird last night. Left the team before they finished searching and had a strange attitude. He's also another one who thought Ritchie got away with his part in the rapes."

"You don't think he—"

"No, but we do have eyes on things. I found out where on the property Ritchie has a line shack, and Hank Patterson has one of his guys settled with binocs keeping an eye on it. Last night, sure enough, Ritchie rode out there on his four-wheeler, and get this. He carried in something that looked like food."

"Well, that nails it," Wolf said. "Why not—"

"Because we want to catch him in the act, like I said. Hank sent a fresh pair of eyes to watch the shack, but we don't want to do anything until it's dark. If they're playing that hunting game, they'll be doing it after dark. The minute Ritchie makes a move we're ready to go. I'm trying to decide how much to tell Lacey before we actually get it done."

Wolf glanced over at her. She was awake now and pushing herself to a sitting position, a frown creasing her forehead.

"What?" she mouthed.

"I think she needs to know what's happening," Wolf told him. "She can handle it. She'd rather know than be kept in the dark."

"Yes, to whatever it is," she said in a soft voice.

"She's in," Wolf said into the phone.

"Okay. Hank and I and a few others will be there in an hour. We'll bring breakfast. We have work to do."

He put the phone on the nightstand and stood up. Lacey was looking at him with a combination of worry and fear in her eyes.

"Please tell me what's going on."

"Alex, Hank Patterson, and a couple of the Brotherhood Protectors will be here in a bit. We may know where your sister and Trace are, but we can't go in with guns blazing or searchlights all over the place."

"Why not? Please, Wolf. Whatever it is, we have to get them."

"Can you hold it together until everyone gets here? Then they'll lay it out for you and answer all your questions."

She looked about ready to explode.

"Until I hear what they have to say. Then all bets are off."

And that was about as good as he was going to get.

"I can live with that. I need to get up."

He cleared his throat. "Do you need any help getting ready?"

Lacey managed a smile. "You say that so delicately. I think I can manage myself. My arm feels much better today. The doctor said if you can wrap it in plastic, I can shower. I think I can handle showering and dressing by myself, but I want to get going. If you can just help me get my stuff ready…"

He was amazed at how smoothly they worked together. They had only known each other for forty-eight hours, but you'd think they'd been doing it forever. He didn't know which of them was more surprised. She shooed him out of the room, insisting she could dress herself and promising to yell if she had a problem.

He showered and dressed in the other bathroom with practiced speed and was ready for whatever when she called out his name.

"I think I need you to do the dressing," she told him.

He noticed most of the swelling had gone down from her arm and she moved it as if the pain was considerably less. He offered her the pain pills, but she refused in favor of two over-the-counter tablets after Wolf changed the dressing.

He felt as if they'd done this forever.

Two days, hotshot. It's only been two days.

But sometimes things happened the way they were supposed to for a reason.

They had just made their way into the kitchen when there was a knock on the front door. Wolf went to open it and, in a minute, Alex, Jesse, Hank, Kujo, and another man they introduced as Sam Franklin filed into the house. Jesse carried two large pastry boxes that he set on the counter.

"Don't worry," he told Wolf who frowned. "We'll need all that sugar for energy, and we'll work it off pretty fast. Load up, guys, and let's get to work."

Wolf insisted on carrying Lacey's coffee and pastry to the table before he got his own. Then, in minutes, they were all seated, and Hank was rolling out another map.

"Okay. I got a look at the map the guy from county had and marked it on here. This is where the line shack is." He pointed with his finger. "It's in the far corner of his ten thousand acres. That acreage converts to a little over fifteen square miles. His hands used it sometimes when they were moving cattle from one area to the other but apparently not for a very long time."

"You think that's where Heather and Trace are? But why?"

"Best place to keep someone. Who knows how many other times he's gotten away with it. Maybe some of the disappearances that haven't been solved are part of that."

"Oh my god." Lacey covered her mouth, looking

as if she might be sick. "If that's it, Heather and Trace could already be gone."

Alex shook his head. "I don't think so. If they were, he wouldn't have brought food out there last night. Lacey, I promise you, Hank and I have eyes on that place every minute."

She slumped in her chair, and Wolf thought it interesting no one gave them a side-eye when he moved closer to her and put his arm around her.

For the next hour, they went over the plans for the evening. During that time, both Alex and Hank took updates on the search parties out working during daylight hours. The effort might be fruitless, but everyone agreed they needed to keep up the image of the search. And who knew what they might stumble over, including things not related to this situation.

Kujo arrived just as they were wrapping things up. He had Six with him, and Wolf had to swallow a smile as Bailey, who'd been sitting right next to Lacey, whined and quivered to greet the other dog.

Wolf chuckled. *"Het is okay."*

Then Bailey startled him by looking at Lacey, who smiled and nodded.

"I think he's adopted you," Kujo commented. "Wolf, you gonna sue her for alienation of affections?"

"No, it's all good." He ignored the looks the others gave him. "More coffee, anyone?"

Kujo filled everyone in on the details of his surveillance of Ritchie's property and the shack itself.

"There was only one person riding the four-wheeler," he told them. "He carried what looked like a tray with food, but he stayed less than five minutes."

"So, if he'd bring them something to eat," Lacey persisted, "then they're still alive. Right?" She looked at the men. "Am I right?"

"Yes." Alex was the one who answered her. "He's keeping them alive, at least until tonight. Hank, we'll rendezvous at your place, get everything ready to go, and then move."

"I want to go with you," Lacey insisted.

Everyone shook their heads.

"It's not safe for you," Wolf told her.

"Plus," Alex added, "there really is nothing for you to do."

"And you're afraid I'd be in the way," she snapped then sighed. "It's just going to be so hard to sit here and wait."

"Lacey, we're all trained in things like this, and I'm sure you don't want to distract us from our mission."

"I just want to make sure Heather and Trace are safe," she cried.

"And we will do that. In fact, I'll keep in constant radio contact with Wolf. I brought a unit for him, and he'll be tuned into our frequency so he is up to date at all times. This baby has a distance of thirty-five miles, so we're good to go."

Wolf saw her deflate at Alex's words.

"Okay. I understand." She wrinkled her forehead. "You think he's the one who shot me?"

"I do. And we'll get him for that, too. And now, we need to get going. We have arrangements to make. And Hank is organizing a little surprise for us."

"Oh?" She sat up straighter and looked at Hank. "What is it?"

"Like he said, it's a surprise. But you'll get to see it after the fact because Kujo will be documenting everything on video."

Everyone said their goodbyes, although Kujo had a hard time getting Six to come along willingly.

"I might sue Bailey for alienation of affections," he joked. "When this is wrapped up, we need to arrange playtime for them."

"I'm good with that," Wolf told him.

He walked everyone to the door then came back to where Lacey still sat at the dining room table, fiddling with her now-cold coffee.

"Want me to freshen that for you?"

She shook her head. "I think the less coffee I drink today the better."

"How's the arm?"

She touched it lightly with her fingertips. "Still sore but doing much better."

"Good. Let me know if you need pain meds though."

Wolf could tell as the hours passed that the day was dragging for Lacey. He was growing impatient himself. He would have liked to be in on the rescue himself, but Lacey couldn't be left unguarded, just in case, and there was no way he was leaving that job to someone else.

Alex called a couple of times during the day to keep them up to date on arrangements. He also let them know that his spotter who was keeping eyes on the shack reported that the four-wheeler had been driven to the shack this morning with what was apparently breakfast. The driver wore a hood over his head, but from his size and build, it was easy to identify him as Ritchie. He'd left the shack, and there had been no activity since then.

Alex also reported that Ritchie had actually come to the sheriff's office to ask if there'd been any word on the missing couple. He'd apologized for not finding anything with his team and offered to volunteer again.

"Although he did say," Alex told him in a grim voice, "that he was only available for part of the evening."

"Asshole." Wolf spat the word.

"That he is."

Wolf tried to get Lacey to lie down in the afternoon, but he finally realized nothing short of hitting her on the head with a baseball bat would get her to do that. He took Bailey out for some exercise, and he brought Lacey outside with him but kept her close to the house. He didn't trust Ritchie, if this really was him, not to try another shot at her.

Neither of them ate very much dinner. Wolf literally had to force Lacey to swallow some canned soup he heated up. He felt helpless because he couldn't think of any way to distract her that wouldn't, at this particular time, be in very poor taste. He even let her watch him do his exercises for his shoulder. But time dragged, as if weighed down by sandbags.

Alex checked in a couple of times to let them know there was still no activity around the shack. As far as they could tell, Ritchie spent most of the day in the ranch house, although he took that one trip into town, checking to see if the search was still going on.

This whole thing was very hard on him. He was not used to sitting on the sidelines, letting other people catch the bad guys. He wanted to be out there with his gun, hoping Cordell Ritchie would twitch the wrong way and he could blow him to hell.

When his phone rang about four o'clock, and he saw Alex's name, he figured he was getting another update on the timeline.

"Still good to go?" he asked.

"Better than that. Grab Lacey and Bailey, and get your ass out in back of the house."

"What? What's going on?" He looked out the big window that faced the extended acreage and frowned.

"We all decided it wasn't right for you to miss the big moment here. I called a friend who has a helicopter. He—"

"Did you say a helicopter?" Was he hearing right?

"I did. Hank and I discussed it and decided that,

for one thing, we needed an attack on two fronts. We want to scare the shit out of these guys and shock them so we can get the hostages away before anyone gets shot. We were afraid Ritchie would do it if we just drove up to the cabin. Also, we can flip on the spotlight and not only blind them for a moment but see our way to rappel down."

"That's—unbelievable. Where did you find one?"

"I have a contact," Hank told him.

"Of course you do." Wolf shook his head.

"Guy used to be a Night Stalker. You know, those guys who provided air support for us SEALs. He'll be landing any minute in back of your house to take the three of you to my place where Micki's waiting for Lacey and Bailey. Hank sent two of his guys to run guard duty there, and I've got a security system that could protect the president. We all figured you deserved to be in on this."

Wolf didn't know what to say. He was totally overcome and so very grateful. Yes, he did indeed want the chance to confront the bastard who'd shot Lacey and captured her family.

"Thanks," was all he could manage.

"You can thank me later. Get going."

"What is it?" Lacey had hurried over to him, fear wild in her eyes. "Did something bad happen?"

"No." He shook his head. "Something good. Come on. We're going for a ride in a chopper."

He made sure she had whatever she needed for

her arm before he hustled her and Bailey outside, where the chopper was just landing.

Bailey gave a short bark.

"Yeah, guy." He grinned. "You've ridden in plenty of these, right?"

He got everyone inside the cabin, and they lifted off even before he had the door slid fully closed.

CHAPTER 13

Wolf tried to curb his impatience as he waited with Alex and his deputies in Jesse's new tricked-out Jeep across from the entrance to the Ritchie property. They'd decided the law should invade the house, disabling the security gate, rather than the Brotherhood Protectors. It would eliminate a lot of after-the-fact blowback. Alex wanted them to wait until Lani Running Bear, one of Hank's Brotherhood Protectors who had taken the current watch, signaled them that the four-wheeler was out again. They had radio contact set up between the two groups so everything could be coordinated.

Just then, the radio crackled.

"They're on the move." Running Bear's voice came over the connection. He was situated in a tree, now, that gave him a wide view. "Two men riding in, in the four-wheeler and heading toward the shack."

"Okay, got it." Alex's radio squawked again, and he pressed a button. "Rossi here."

Now it was Hank's voice that came over the connection, from the chopper. "We're ready here. That four-wheeler's getting close."

"Is he paying attention to you?"

"Negative. I had the chopper do a few flybys today, so he wouldn't think it was strange. Time to get to it."

"We're rolling. Give us a few to get close enough."

The Jeep pulled up to the gates that led to the ranch house, stopping by the electronic security box. Jesse pulled out a small metal unit that he told Wolf was an electromagnetic pulse unit. It could emit a short burst of energy strong enough to kill the electronics in the call box and open the gates. Zane hopped out and pushed on the gates and, sure enough, they opened. In seconds, they were past the house and headed out across the vast acreage toward where they knew the shack was. Jesse's new four-wheel-drive truck ate up the landscape.

Alex's radio squawked again.

"Ritchie and the guy with him are at the shack," Hank said. "And damn! I think that's Bryson Hall, vice president of the bank! Well, fuck. That ought to make a big mess."

"We're almost there," Alex told him.

"Ritchie just opened the door to the shack and brought a man and woman outside. I've got the binocs on them. And, Alex? They look to be in pretty rough shape."

Wolf's stomach clenched with dread.

"Okay," Alex said into the radio. "Go for it."

One second later, bright searchlights flooded the area. Wolf could see four people caught in its circle and, right near them, four men fast-roping down to the ground.

Hank, Kujo, and two other Protectors fast-roped down into the pasture surrounding the shack. By then the Jeep had swirled to a stop, and everyone was out of it. Ritchie and the man with him were temporarily blinded by the spotlight, but then, in a second, Ritchie grabbed the woman Wolf was sure was Heather Cooper. He backed away, looking wildly at the men closing in.

"Let her go," Wolf hollered, leveling his .45 at the man.

"Shoot me, and I'll shoot her," he growled.

"Heather?" the other prisoner, who had to be Trace, called out the woman's name.

Wolf thought the man looked as if he might pass out, even as he tried to break free from one of Hank's men who was holding him back.

"Oh god," he cried, "please don't shoot her. She's been through enough."

"Cordell?" His friend, Bryce, was being restrained by Hank. "Cordell, we need to find a way out of this."

"I've got this."

"No, you don't. I don't want to die for this. That

wasn't in the plan. For god's sake, please don't shoot anyone."

"You want out of this, don't you?"

The pilot had adjusted the spotlight so Wolf was no longer in its circle. Wolf watched Hank move forward toward Ritchie and Heather, drawing the man's attention from anything else. The others were moving around him, too, trying to prevent him from squeezing the trigger. Hoping to distract him as they looked for opportunities to get that gun moved from Heather's temple.

Wolf lowered himself into a crouch and slid around just outside the circle, beyond the spotlight, until he was in back of Cordell Ritchie. He moved slowly up until he was right behind the man and, in a fluid movement, stuck the barrel of his gun in the man's ear.

"Make one fucking move, one twitch of your finger," he growled, "and I'll put a hole in your head from side to side."

He watched Ritchie's hand tremble and, when that gun had eased a little from Heather, Wolf grabbed it and yanked it in the opposite direction. From the corner of his eye, he saw Hank and Alex restrain Ritchie and handcuff him. Heather was trembling uncontrollably in his arms, so he pulled her against his body and tried to soothe her.

"I've got her." Alex appeared next to him and grabbed the woman, who appeared on the verge of collapse. "We need to get her to the hospital ASAP.

And take the guy, too. Trace, right? He doesn't look much better."

"We'll take them on the chopper," Hank told him and spoke into the radio in his hand. "Wolf, you want to go with them, too? And Kujo will go along, just in case. I can call Lacey and have the helo come back to get her and transport her there, too."

Wolf nodded. He would have demanded to be on the helo if necessary. "Thank you. I mean, really, thanks."

As the chopper pulled away, Wolf observed the activity below: wrestling Ritchie and his friend into the Jeep, checking the shack and taking pictures of the inside, the Jeep heading toward the front end of the property with Alex, Jesse, Kujo, and the two bastards. The Protectors piling into the four-wheeler and following the Jeep.

Then he looked over at Heather and Trace, bruised and scratched and filthy dirty, and looking as if they'd been to hell and back. They were seated in the back of the chopper, and Zane, who was flying with them, helping them drink from bottles of water.

And he took out his phone.

"Hi, Heather. I'm Wolf Makalski. I'm a friend of your sister's. She'll be damn glad to see that we've got you two. In a minute, I'll have someone on the phone who's going to be very happy to talk to you."

"M-My sister?"

He nodded. "I'm calling her right now."

He punched in Lacey's number. She answered on the first ring. "Do you have her? Is she okay?"

"Ask her yourself."

And he handed over the phone.

He tried not to listen to the conversation, but Heather was crying so hard, she could barely talk. Trace reached a shaky hand over and squeezed her arm, which helped a little. Wolf took the phone back from her.

"Lacey? We're almost to the hospital. Then the pilot will be back to pick you up."

"I can go see her? Right now?"

"That's the plan. Bailey will hang out at the Kuntz's with Six."

There was a long pause, and he wondered if for some reason she'd hung up, but then he heard her voice again, weak with relief.

"Wolf?"

"Yeah, babe?" *Babe?* Where the hell had that come from?

"Thank you, Just…thank you."

"I was just part of the group. Okay, I'm hanging up now, but get ready for your ride."

When they landed on the roof of the hospital, several people in scrubs rushed out. Seconds later, they had transferred Heather and Trace to stretchers and whisked them inside.

"We're taking them to emergency," one of them called back to the chopper.

Zane thanked the pilot then grabbed Wolf's arm

and headed inside. Wolf thought it was a good thing Zane remembered how to navigate from the other night because his mind sure wasn't on following a bunch of corridors and trying to find where they'd taken Heather and Trace.

Finally, Zane just grabbed his arm and said, "This way."

When they reached emergency, Zane used his badge to power his way past everyone and be shown to where Heather and Trace were being treated. Wolf breathed a sigh of relief when neither the doctor nor the nurse taking care of them made them leave the room or gave them an argument about anything. The nurse did pull the curtain around Heather while she removed her clothes and bathed her.

Wolf had only gotten a quick view of them when the chopper flew them to the hospital, but what he saw made him want to throw up. And it wasn't just her. Both she and Trace look like they'd dropped some weight, and their skin was covered with scrapes and scratches and cuts.

Wolf leaned against one wall in the hallway but kept an eye on what was happening while the medical staff did their things.

"She has some badly infected cuts," one of the nurses told him when she stepped out from behind the curtain to get some supplies. "She's lucky she didn't develop septicemia."

Wolf's stomach knotted at those words. He'd seen

septic wounds in the battlefield when it wasn't possible to transport the injured right away.

"I'm just glad we were able to get them out of where they were when we did."

"Who would let something like that happen to people?" She shook her head as she left the room.

"Listen, I'm going downstairs to grab a coffee," Zane told him. "Can I bring you one?"

Wolf shook his head. "I'm good. But you don't need to hang around here. I know you've got things to do."

Zane barked a rough laugh. "That's no lie. The minute word gets out that Cordell Ritchie and his friend are booked into the jail, this county is going to explode. Okay. One of Hank's Brotherhood Protectors agents is choppering here with Lacey. Send him down to me when he gets here, which should be any minute, and I'll give him a ride back."

Both Heather and Trace were still being worked on when Lacey arrived with one of the Brotherhood Protectors who'd been doing guard duty at Alex and Micki's house. She blew right past Wolf and into the area where her sister was, ignoring what was going on.

"I know, I know," she said to whoever was trying to move her. "But my sister nearly died, so give me a minute, okay? I wasn't sure I'd ever see her alive again."

Wolf hung back in the hallway with Hank's man whose name was Sam Franklin.

"Micki decided it was a bad move to send her on the chopper by herself," the man told Alex. "She was holding it together pretty good, but you could tell she was carrying a heavy load of stress."

"No, you're right," Wolf agreed. "She didn't need to be alone on that chopper."

"But now that she's delivered, and you're here with her, I'll catch a ride back home. I understand Zane's here?"

Wolf nodded. "Downstairs. He said he'd be waiting for you. Listen, thanks for everything, all of you."

Sam shrugged. "It's what we do."

Hank will be in touch as soon as he finishes cleaning up the nasty business at that shack." Sam shook his head. "It's hard to believe the things some humans do to others."

"Amen to that."

"Anyway, I'm outta here. Hank will update you on everything when he gets here."

As soon as Sam walked away, Wolf headed into the examination room. All the privacy curtains were pulled back now. Heather and Trace both looked as if they'd been cleaned and had their wounds treated, and both were receiving IV saline solutions. Lacey was standing next to her sister, but she turned the moment Wolf came back into the room and literally threw herself at him.

"I'll never be able to thank you." She buried her face against his chest.

"Just getting them out of there is thanks enough," he assured her.

She'd planted herself against his chest and wrapped her arms around him. He could feel tears soaking his shirt, and he wished like hell he was better at comforting people. Not to mention the fact his body was telling him it wanted more of her.

Just what she needs right now, asshole.

She finally stepped back, pulled a handkerchief out of her jeans pocket, and wiped her eyes.

"Sorry." She sniffed. "Didn't mean to fall apart all over you."

"Hey. You've been through an emotional ordeal. It's okay. I get it."

She took his hand and tugged him toward her sister.

"Come meet Heather. She wants to thank you herself."

"Oh, Lacey, I don't know. She's not in great shape right now."

"But she and Trace are alive because of you and Alex and his men and the Brotherhood Protectors," she reminded him. "Please. She really wants to."

Heather was dressed in a hospital gown and lying on a bed, a pillow beneath her head. Someone had brushed her shoulder-length, dark-brown hair. She was so pale, her skin looked almost stark white, and Wolf could still see vestiges of fear in her eyes. Once again, rage surged through him. If Cordell Ritchie had been in front of him at the moment, he would have beaten the man black-and-blue.

The nurse finished applying antiseptic ointment to cuts and scrapes.

"You'll need stitches in some of these," she was telling Heather, "and the doctor is going to give you a shot of antibiotics to fight off infection. But you're looking better already. You're getting saline solution intravenously, but try to drink as much water as you can, also. You're pretty dehydrated."

She stepped away, and Lacey urged Wolf closer to the bed.

Heather gave him a weak smile.

"I don't know how we'll ever thank you." Her voice was still weak, but she managed a smile. "Every night, they threatened to kill us but I think tonight they

were planning to do it for real. I couldn't—"

She stopped as tears leaked from her eyes.

"We can talk about that when you're feeling better. For now, what's important is you're safe and being cared for." He grinned. "The person you really want to thank is Lacey, who's a real bulldog."

"And we're damn glad of it." The heavy masculine voice came from the other bed.

"Trace wants to thank you, too," Heather told him. "Please?"

"She's right. We owe you our lives."

Lacey gave him a gentle shove in the direction of the bed where Trace was lying. The man lying there was close to six feet, mostly muscle. His black hair was thick and slightly tangled, and a dark, overgrown scruff beard highlighted his face. His eyes were ebony, and Wolf thought they'd probably be full of life under normal circumstances. Now they bore a haunted look, *like Heather's*. And he was hooked to a bag of saline solution like Heather.

"The person you really owe," he told Trace, "is your sister-in-law. When she wants something done, there's no stopping her."

Trace managed that rough laugh again. "And aren't we glad of it."

"She wouldn't give up," Wolf went on. "Buttonholed every single person she thought could be of any help."

"Too many people wanted to write it off as another missing person in the Crazy Mountains." Lacey shook her head. "But I know you guys aren't stupid enough to go wandering off in these mountains in places where it's easy to disappear."

"And we didn't, which is the weird thing. We were having dessert and coffee in a diner when a man sitting next to us struck up a conversation." He shifted slightly on the bed. "They locked us up like animals."

Before anyone could say anything else, Alex Rossi walked into the exam room.

"Everything okay so far in here?" he asked.

"Seems to be," Wolf told him. "Still a lot to do, but at least we have them safe and sound and under good care. But don't you have a circus going on down at your jail?"

"The state police came and picked our dirtbags up. They'll hand them over to the FBI. Kidnapping's a federal charge. These guys are going to wish they'd never thought up their little game."

"Well, then, come in and meet two grateful people."

Alex introduced himself to Heather and Trace.

"I am so sorry for whatever you've all been through. Do either of you feel up to giving me any details of what happened?"

"I will." Trace's voice was filled with venom. "I want those bastards stuck away in the deepest hole you can find."

"How did you meet them?"

"By being gullible tourists. We'd been here more than a week, camping at different places. Trying to talk Lacey into coming out and joining us. We were having coffee and pie in a diner one afternoon, and I was running off at the mouth about how I'd like to see one of these big ranches here. Get a firsthand look at it. I guess I'm a frustrated cowboy."

"Nothing wrong with that," Alex told him. "A lot of people who come out here are just that."

"But lucky for them, they don't meet up with assholes like this." He paused to take a drink of water. "Anyway, they overheard me, and the bigger one invited us to his ranch. Can you believe I still don't know their fucking names? He told me to call him

Hunter. We soon enough found out why." He paused, closing his eyes for a moment.

"I think I know why, but I'd like to hear it from you."

"They hunted us." He spat the words out. "Like animals. They kept us locked in that ratty cabin with a slop bucket, bottles of water, and food twice a day. Late at night, they'd let us out and tell us to get going. They'd give us a head start then be off to hunt us down. Tracking us like animals."

"Oh my god." Lacey's whisper carried throughout the room.

Trace hauled in another breath then let it out slowly. "We had until it started to get light. They only hunted in the dark. As long as we didn't get caught, we got to live another day."

Wolf could hear sobbing coming from behind him, and he assumed it was Heather. Who could blame her? A nightmare like this was going to take a long time to recover from.

"We can leave this for now, if you want to," Alex said.

"No." Trace's voice was edged with bitterness. "I want to get it all on the table now before those vermin find a way to weasel out of it."

"That's not gonna happen," Alex assured him, "but okay. Keep going, as long as you can."

"They split us up. We had to run separately. Not stay together. They had us in a part of the ranch that's all overgrown with bushes and shrubs and different trees. I at least had long pants on, but Heather was wearing shorts. Her legs are a mess. Anyway, every night we made it through, hiding, not getting caught, we got to live another day. But I knew we were getting close to the end of their patience. I thought I might have found a way out of there."

"A way out?" Alex cocked his head. "But that section of the property has a cyclone fence around it. We shorted out the gate then pushed it open and drove on through. Jeep. How else could you get out of there?"

"There's a tree at one corner of the metal fencing. I'd finally figured out a way to climb it. Tonight, I was going to have Heather circle around and meet me so I could try to get both of us out of there." He almost managed a smile. "Then the cavalry arrived."

"And thank god," Heather added.

And then, as if the last of her control had shattered, she broke into shuddering sobs.

"Okay," Lacey snapped. "That's enough for now."

"Yes, it is." Trace tried to lift himself up from the position he'd been lying in.

"Hey. What's going on?" The ER doctor walked into the room, and Wolf saw him look from one person to another and then another. "Okay, that's it. Everyone out but my patients."

Lacey planted herself firmly next to her sister. "I'm not leaving, so don't even think of trying to throw me out. My sister's been through a horrendous ordeal, and I'm staying right here."

Wolf had to swallow a laugh. Lacey Cooper was definitely a take-no-shit woman. If they hadn't been surrounded by people, he would have wrapped her up in a big hug. And that surprised him more than anything else.

The doctor looked around as if waiting for someone to help him then heaved a sigh. "Fine, but everyone else out until I'm finished here." When no one moved, he snapped, "Now!"

Wolf gave Trace's shoulder a guy squeeze and mouthed the words, "Not leaving," before following Alex out into the hall.

"This is some welcome we gave you," Alex joked. "It continues to amaze me what goes on beneath the surface in what looks like an idyllic corner of the world. That whole episode with the rapes, that actually spanned a few years, shocked the shit out of me, but after that nothing surprises me."

"So, did these guys say anything? Give you any idea why they cooked this up?"

Alex shook his head. "Ritchie cussed us out royally and threatened everything but cutting off our dicks, but he shut up when he saw we weren't letting him go. Guy Ferman about wet his pants, but Ritchie told him to shut it, that he'd take care of things. I assume when they got to the state police facility, he called an attorney. Thank fuck they're someone else's problem now."

"No kidding."

"So, if we haven't scared you off, you think you

might take that position as one of my deputies? I'm going to text you all the details with salary and benefits, which includes the option on that house. Which, by the way, you've hardly had time to enjoy. Don't say anything now. Just think it over. I'll be in touch. Meanwhile, I think Lacey is going to need you for the next few days."

He sure as hell hoped so, which continued to surprise him.

"Sounds good. And, Alex? Thanks for everything."

The sheriff nodded and walked away down the corridor.

CHAPTER 14

Lacey looked up from her tablet at Wolf who had just walked onto the back porch with mugs of fresh coffee and set them on the table. Bailey, who was lying down beside her, perked up his ears then rested his head again on his paws. She knew Wolf was stunned at how well she and the dog had bonded, but he kept telling her how glad he was and that it was a sign. They had yet to discuss that sign.

"This whole thing is certainly a nine-days wonder." It had actually been more than two weeks since they'd found Trace and Heather and rescued them.

"Well, damn," he said, taking the seat next to her. "I guess so. Alex called earlier, while you were in the shower. You know, he's got that list of people who disappeared in this particular area over the past five years. He got the state out there with their ground-penetrating radar because he had a feeling they're buried on the Ritchie property."

"Have they had any luck?"

"Sadly, yes. They've recovered four skeletons so far. They'll keep looking, but they've already got two top-notch forensic anthropologists working on them. And, of course, the relatives of people who disappeared are banging on his doors and the doors of the states. And every media outlet you can name is jonesing for the story."

"Oh god." Lacey put her tablet on the table and took a long swallow of her coffee. "I never imagined when I came out here to look for Heather and Trace that it would turn into this."

"I don't think anyone did."

"Did you know he told them to call him Hunter?" She shook her head. "That is so revolting."

"I agree. But Heather and Trace seem to be doing well."

After three days in the hospital, they'd come to stay with Lacey and Wolf, mostly keeping to themselves and doing their best to heal. Today, the other couple had decided to venture out into the world for a little while just in the immediate area.

"I agree. It's so sad because I know they had actually texted me they thought they might move here."

Wolf shrugged. "Give them some time to heal. They might change their minds. We can talk to them and see if that's still a possibility. I'd hate for one vermin infecting the area to ruin it for them."

"Me, too. But don't forget. They'll still have that trial to get through first, and all the testifying." She shook her head. "That's going to be an ordeal for them, and we don't even know when it's going to take place. They have an appointment to be interviewed by the FBI day after tomorrow, so maybe they'll know something then."

"Let's hope Ritchie's high-priced lawyers don't drag this out for months. He's got plenty of money to pay them."

"Damn." She shook her head. "Don't even suggest that."

"Listen. Just in the short time I've known Heather and Trace, they seem like two very strong people. Of course, they had to be to get through their ordeal. But they have each other and, as a couple, they are even stronger."

"I'm just giving them space to heal and figure out what's next for them."

Wolf took Lacey's hand in his and gave it a gentle squeeze. "And can I ask what's next for you, Miss Lacey Cooper?"

She smiled at him, a feeling of warmth curling in her stomach as she saw the heat in his eyes.

"Well," she sighed, drawing the word out, "first I need to make sure my sister is on the right path again. Then I have to figure out what *my* path is."

"And do you know where you want it to go?"

She looked down at where his hand was holding hers.

"I want to see," she told him, "if what's going on between us is more than just a physical exercise. What about you?"

"I never thought I'd be saying this, but I want it, too." He lifted her hand and kissed the back of it. "I was such a mess when I left the SEALs. My life was one color. Black. Alex's offer was like a lifeline to me. Then I met you, a connection totally unexpected. And everything just took off from there."

"You're thinking of taking Alex's offer."

"It depends."

"On?"

"What the deal is with us." He pointed to her then to himself. "We've been dancing around this ever since I overstepped the day we arrived at this house. I—"

"No," she interrupted, "you didn't. Did I tell you to stop? Put up barriers?"

He shook his head. "But—"

"But so much has come down since that moment," she reminded him.

"It has," he agreed. "Your arm still doing okay?"

"It is." She'd had the stitches taken out a couple of days ago, and the doctor pronounced the arm in good shape. It was still a little tender, but the analgesic cream they gave her really helped on that score.

"My arm healing. Looking for Heather and Trace. Finding them in that unspeakable situation. Getting them through those first few days." "And now, here we are. Lacey, I want to see if we've got what I think we do. Fair warning. I haven't had this kind of connection, this kind of desire, in a very long time. I'm not even sure how good I am at it anymore."

"Oh, well." She smiled. "I'll bet you're a lot better than you think you are."

"Then, I think we should discuss it." He rose and held a hand out to her. "Privately."

Bailey rose from the floor and padded after them as Wolf led her into the bedroom she'd been using, the one where he'd cared for her so gently and with such concern.

"Not this time, boy," Wolf told him. "Some things are best done in private."

Bailey looked at them and whined.

"Oh, for god's sake." Wolf crouched down and took the dog's face in his palms. "I love you, but this isn't your playtime, buddy. *Blijven.*"

Stay.

The he tugged Lacey into the bedroom.

She laughed when he turned the lock in the door. "We're the only ones here."

"Trace and Heather won't be out doing whatever it is they're doing forever." He brushed a kiss over her lips. "And Bailey's learned how to turn knobs. I don't believe in taking chances, at least not with this."

They'd had only had stolen moments of intimacy since they'd found Trace and Heather. Her arm was still healing, plus she'd been too caught up in making sure her sister recovered. But, the last few days, that intimacy had grown until just scratching the surface had become not enough. Now her arm was healed, and they had the house to themselves, and her body was hungry for him. Her nipples ached, her sex throbbed, and every nerve was screaming.

She started to unbutton her blouse, but he brushed her hands away.

"Let me."

He took his time doing it, sliding the blouse from her shoulders and down her arms. He tossed it to the little chair against the wall then cupped her breasts nestled in the satin bra and licked the swells with slow sweeps of his tongue. Shivers skittered down her spine at his touch, and she gripped his forearms to steady herself. He took his time, tasting and licking before reaching behind her to open the clasp. The bra fell away, and Wolf cupped her naked breasts in his warm palms.

"True confession." His voice was hoarse and tentative. "Since my injury I haven't been with a woman for more than a temporary physical exercise. I'm afraid I forgot how to do this right."

She gave a shaky laugh. "As far as I'm concerned there is no wrong way. Wolf, I haven't been with anyone in ages, and my last relationship was a disaster. You have no place to go here but up."

"I hope so."

The he bent his head and sucked a nipple into his mouth.

Lacey felt it harden immediately, and heat shot straight to her sex, her inner walls spasming with instant need, and she could already feel the dampness of her juices. He pulled hard on the suddenly pebbled tip, lightly biting it before giving the same attention to the other one. He kneaded her breasts as he sucked and nipped and scraped his teeth over her tender flesh.

Heat was streaking through her and she had to touch him. She grabbed the hem of his T-shirt and yanked it up.

"Get rid of this," she told him. "Now."

His laugh was low and guttural. "I like a woman who gives orders."

He dragged the T-shirt over his head and tossed it to the chair on top of her bra. Lacey reached up and ran her hand over the muscles of his shoulder that still bore faint scars. Those muscles were harder than the others she touched as she glided her palm over his back and down his spine.

He tensed while she did it, but when she ran her tongue over his chest, flicking the tip against his own nipples, she felt tension easing from his body. And she felt the tension in her own body shifting and taking on a new feel.

Wolf strung kisses along her chin and down her neck before drawing a line with his tongue down the valley between her breasts. His hands traced the rest of her curves as he unzipped her jeans and eased them down her legs. In seconds, the rest of her clothing was gone, along with her shoes.

Then he cupped her chin and stared directly into her eyes.

"I think I'll do this a lot better if we're lying down."

He didn't wait for her to say anything, just lifted her in his arms and reached down to strip back the quilt and sheet on her bed and placed her with her head on the pillow. Then he just stood a moment, his gaze traveling over every inch of her body. Every nerve she owned was firing and her sex was wet with anticipation. When he licked his lips, she was afraid she might just come then and there.

"Gorgeous," he murmured. "Incredible."

"I want to see you, too," she told him.

He never took his eyes from her as he toed off his shoes and yanked his socks. Next came his jeans and his boxer briefs, which he tossed onto the pile of their clothing. When his cock sprang free, every bit of moisture in her mouth dried up.

Holy mother!

Every inch of him was hard muscle, beautifully sculpted despite the evidence of his injuries. But it was his magnificent cock that made her nearly combust. Long and thick, with a dark-purple head that at the moment sported a tiny drop of fluid on the crown. Below it, his balls hung thick against his thighs. She couldn't help running her tongue over her lips and wishing she was tasting something else.

Apparently Wolf had the same idea because he climbed onto the bed, nudging her thighs apart so he could kneel between them. Then, after a long look that set every nerve on fire, he began to run his tongue over every inch of her. He moved his mouth from her neck to her breasts, pausing to nip each of her painfully hard nipples before moving down to her navel. With the tip of his tongue, he traced the furled flesh, sending a shiver through her.

He used his big hands to urge her thighs farther apart, bending her legs at the knee so she was spread wide open to his attention.

"Gorgeous," he murmured.

Then, with his thumbs, he spread the lips of her sex apart, exposing every inch of her to him, bent his head, and took a long, slow lick of her sex. Heat shot straight from her core through the rest of her body, and her pulse rate zoomed up the scale. Then he did it again. And again. When he closed his teeth over her clit and tugged, she nearly came off the bed.

"You're so fucking responsive," he growled, and did it again.

"Better be careful," she warned, breathlessly. "I might come before it's time."

"Sugar, you can come as many times as you want. It will be my pleasure."

As he said that, his voice low and rich, he slid two fingers into her slick-and-waiting body.

Oh god!

She clamped down on them and tried to ride them. Gripping his upper arms so hard, her nails dug into his skin.

"That good, sugar?" His voice was low and rough.

"Better than good. But I want my turn, too."

He looked down at her and raised an eyebrow. "I thought I was giving you your turn."

She reached down between them and found his cock, so hard and thick and throbbing.

"I want this," she told him.

"You've got it."

"But I want it in my hands and in my mouth and…"

He covered her lips with his hand. "Shh. We've got plenty of time for all of that. But if I don't get inside you right now, I might expire." He reached into the nightstand drawer. "I put some supplies in here earlier. Just in case."

He lifted out a string of three condoms, pulled one off, and rolled it on with one hand. Then, adjusting her so she was totally open to him, he pressed the head of his dick to her opening. He stopped after a minute and looked at her again.

"Still okay?"

"Yes," she answered in a breathy voice, "but it won't be if you don't quit teasing me."

"Okay, then. Here I come."

He thrust into her in one swift move, filling her completely. Then he pulled back and pushed in again. He repeated the movement, picking up speed each time, until he was driving into her hard and fast, his thumb rubbing her clit.

The orgasm roared up from deep inside her, so

hard she almost couldn't wait for him. They exploded together, her inner walls clenching and milking him, her body shaking with the spasms. She had no idea how long it went on, only that everything disappeared but the two of them and the intense pleasure that rocked her world.

Finally, the shuddering eased, and she lay there, her inner muscle still clenched around her, wondering how she'd survive this intense pleasure.

Wolf brushed his lips over hers. "That was…unbelievable. I hope it was for you, too."

She gave a breathy little laugh. "Are you kidding? It was…earthshattering."

He kissed her again.

"Lacey, maybe I should wait until we're both not naked to bring this up, but I want to take this job with Alex. I feel good about myself here and about what I can accomplish. But…"

She frowned. "But what?"

"But I'll turn it down if I can't get you to stay here with me. In a very short time, you've become way more important to me. You make me want to live life again."

Her heart was thumping so hard, she wondered if he could hear it. She'd known it would come to this. Was she ready for this? This kind of relationship? He'd come to mean as much to her and, while she worried it happened too fast, inside she knew she had to do this.

"So, I can work anywhere. I'm not tied to an

office. And I love this place despite the terrible things that happened here."

"Is that a yes?"

She reached up and brought his face down to hers. "That's a very big yes. I don't know what Heather and Trace are going to do but that can't affect our decisions."

"We'll both help them with the residual effects of the trauma, and maybe they'll stay, too." He pressed his mouth to hers, his tongue sliding in and seeking hers as he kissed the breath out of her.

"You won't be sorry," he promised.

She smiled. "I don't believe I will."

At that moment, a loud bark sounded just outside the bedroom door.

"That dog." Wolf shook his head. "We'd better let him in. Heather and Trace will be back soon anyway, and I'd better call Alex and tell him he's got a new deputy." He gave her another kiss. "But later..." His voice trailed off.

"Later," she agreed.

And forever.

ABOUT DESIREE HOLT

USA Today best-selling and award-winning author **Desiree Holt** writes everything from romantic suspense and contemporary on a variety of heat levels up to erotic, a genre in which she is the oldest living author. She has been referred to by *USA Today* as the Nora Roberts of erotic romance, and is a winner of the EPIC E-Book Award, the Holt Medallion and a Romantic Times Reviewers Choice nominee. She has been featured on *CBS Sunday Morning* and in *The Village Voice, The Daily Beast, USA Today, The (London) Daily Mail, The New Delhi Times* and numerous other national and international publications.

Desiree loves to hear from readers.

www.facebook.com/desireeholtauthor
www.facebook.com/desiree01holt
Twitter @desireeholt
Pinterest: desiree02holt
Google: https://g.co/kgs/6vgLUu
www.desireeholt.com
www.desiremeonly.com

Follow Her On:

Amazon
https://www.amazon.com/Desiree-Holt/e/B003LD2Q3M/ref=sr_tc_2_0?qid=1505488204&sr=1-2-ent

Signup for her newsletter
http://eepurl.com/ce7DeE

facebook.com/desiree01holt
twitter.com/desireeholt

BROTHERHOOD PROTECTORS
ORIGINAL SERIES BY ELLE JAMES

Brotherhood Protectors Series
Montana SEAL (#1)
Bride Protector SEAL (#2)
Montana D-Force (#3)
Cowboy D-Force (#4)
Montana Ranger (#5)
Montana Dog Soldier (#6)
Montana SEAL Daddy (#7)
Montana Ranger's Wedding Vow (#8)
Montana SEAL Undercover Daddy (#9)
Cape Cod SEAL Rescue (#10)
Montana SEAL Friendly Fire (#11)
Montana SEAL's Mail-Order Bride (#12)
SEAL Justice (#13)
Ranger Creed (#14)
Delta Force Rescue (#15)
Dog Days of Christmas (#16)
Montana Rescue (Sleeper SEAL)
Hot SEAL Salty Dog (SEALs in Paradise)
Hot SEAL Hawaiian Nights (SEALs in Paradise)
Hot SEAL Bachelor Party (SEALs in Paradise)

Hot SEAL, Independence Day (SEALs in Paradise)

ABOUT ELLE JAMES

ELLE JAMES also writing as MYLA JACKSON is a *New York Times* and *USA Today* Bestselling author of books including cowboys, intrigues and paranormal adventures that keep her readers on the edges of their seats. With over one hundred and eighty works in a variety of sub-genres and lengths she has published with Harlequin, Samhain, Ellora's Cave, Kensington, Cleis Press, and Avon. When she's not at her computer, she's traveling, reading or riding her ATV, dreaming up new stories. Learn more about Elle James at www.ellejames.com

Website | Facebook | Twitter | GoodReads | Newsletter | BookBub | Amazon

Follow Elle!
www.ellejames.com
ellejames@ellejames.com

facebook.com/ellejamesauthor
twitter.com/ElleJamesAuthor

Made in the USA
Columbia, SC
19 April 2022